Help us Rate this book...
Put your initials on the
Left side and your rating
on the right side.
1 = Didn't care for
2 = It was O.K.
3 = It was great

JHK   1 ②3
Rn   1 2 ③
NB   1 2 ③
LR   1 2 ③
mc   1 2 ③
DV   1 2 ③
_____ 1 2 3
_____ 1 2 3
_____ 1 2 3
_____ 1 2 3
_____ 1 2 3
_____ 1 2 3
_____ 1 2 3
_____ 1 2 3

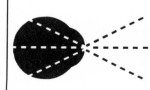

This Large Print Book carries the
Seal of Approval of N.A.V.H.

A NEW JOY

SUSAN PAGE DAVIS

THORNDIKE PRESS
A part of Gale, Cengage Learning

GALE
CENGAGE Learning™

Detroit • New York • San Francisco • New Haven, Conn • Waterville, Maine • London

GALE
CENGAGE Learning·

LIBRARY OF CONGRESS CATALOGING-IN-PUBLICATION DATA

Davis, Susan Page.
    A new joy / by Susan Page Davis. — Large print ed.
        p. cm. — (Thorndike Press large print Christian romance)
    ISBN-13: 978-1-4104-2227-9 (alk. paper)
    ISBN-10: 1-4104-2227-5 (alk. paper)
    1. Large type books. 2. Widows—Fiction. 3. Kidnapping—Fiction. 4. Native Americans—Fiction. I. Title.
PS3604.A976N49 2010
813'.6—dc22   2009040303

Published in 2010 by arrangement with Barbour Publishing, Inc.

Printed in the United States of America
1 2 3 4 5 6 7 14 13 12 11 10

To Lydia,
my sweet granddaughter.
We delight in watching you
grow and learn.

A NOTE FROM THE AUTHOR

I love to hear from my readers! You may correspond with me by writing:

Susan Page Davis
Author Relations
PO Box 721
Uhrichsville, OH 44683

ONE

December 1694

Jane Miller clung to the hands of a child on each side of her and stepped out into the parson's deep footprints in the snow. The biting wind tore at the shawl that partly shielded her face, and the only illumination came from the stars glimmering between clouds overhead.

"I don't want to go," four-year-old Constance Jewett whimpered.

Jane realized that while she stepped in the impressions made by their father's boots, the little girls had to wade through the unbroken snow. The new accumulation of six inches was too much for them.

"It's cold," said Abby.

Jane squeezed the child's fingers with her mittened hand. She could hear Abby's teeth chattering already. A gust of wind blew loose snow in a swirl around them, blinding her for a moment, and Jane stood still until it eased and she could once more make out the footprints in the eerie, blue-white landscape.

The Reverend Samuel Jewett turned and surveyed them. In his arms was his youngest daughter, Ruth, not yet two years old, wrapped in a blanket. His nine-year-old son, John, plodded on and managed to find the deepest drifts.

"Let me carry Constance, as well," the parson said.

Jane trudged the few paces toward him, pulling Constance along. Their long skirts brushed the heavy snow.

Constance let out a shriek. "My shoe! My shoe!"

Jane stooped to lift her. "I'm afraid she got snow in her shoe top."

Constance's layers of winter clothing and thick woolen cloak weighed her down. Jane stumbled the last step as the pastor came to meet her.

He hefted Constance against his shoulder and straightened. "There now, don't fuss, Constance. I'll do well to carry you and Ruthie all the way to Heards' garrison."

"I want Mama." Constance burrowed her face into her father's shoulder as the wind rose once more, cutting through their layers of clothing.

The parson threw Jane a sympathetic look. "I fear we're out on the coldest night of the year. No help for it, though. Keep Abby close." He turned and stalked off, taking slow, deliberate steps.

Jane squeezed Abigail's hand again. "Hold the edge of my cloak and come behind me, Abby. I shall try to stomp the path down for you."

Young John had plowed ahead, and Pastor Jewett called to him to wait. Even in the village, it wasn't wise to let a child run out of sight. Too many young ones had been captured by Indians and hauled off to Canada from the small villages of New Hampshire. Day or night, whether working the cornfields or walking to church, the colonists knew they were never safe. Though the biting cold this last week of December would probably keep the savages away, attacks had occasionally happened even in the dead of winter.

Jane shuddered at the memories triggered by her grim thoughts. Her own time in Canada was a part of her life she would rather forget. She turned her attention back to her task of making a path for the little girl behind her. The moon was down, and she thought they must not be more than an hour from sunrise, but she couldn't be sure.

As they neared the river, the pastor stopped, and Jane pulled up short behind him. A shadowy figure appeared before them, dark against the starlit snow. Jane's heart leaped into her throat. She held back her scream and felt quickly to be sure Abby stayed hidden behind her.

The two little ones in the pastor's arms stayed quiet, but the reverend called out, "Ho, there!"

"Good morn, Reverend," came a hearty voice.

"Oh, Gardner, I didn't recognize you."

The relief in the pastor's voice prompted Jane to peer around him. Her gaze settled on the tall man coming toward them, and she decided it was indeed Charles Gardner, whose farm lay on the outskirts of the village. His bushy beard, bulging pack, and thick winter coat and hat made him appear much bulkier than normal.

"Why are you afoot so early?" Jewett asked.

"I've a trapline along the river here. But where is your family bound?"

"My wife's time has come. I've sent my eldest boy, Ben, to fetch Goody Baldwin. Miss Miller and I are trying to get the other children to Heards' garrison to stay until after the birthing."

Charles Gardner's gaze took in the pastor and his double burden, young John hovering at his father's side, and Jane and Abigail in the rear. "But your wife —"

"Christine Hardin is with her," Jane said quickly then wondered if she should have kept quiet and let the pastor tell his own tale. But they must hurry and get back. Christine was no doubt terrified, being there alone with a woman about to give birth. Goody Jewett had assured her husband there was time to fetch the midwife and disperse the children, but still . . . Things didn't always go the way the mother anticipated.

"Let me help you," Charles said.

"There's no need —," the pastor began.

But Charles cut him off. "Nonsense. It's freezing. Let me carry one of the children, and we'll travel quickly to the garrison. Miss Miller can go back and help with your wife until Goody Baldwin arrives."

"If you're sure . . ."

Charles answered the minister by striding quickly to Jane's side and stooping to address Abby.

Jane wondered that the Reverend Jewett would allow the young man the villagers called wild and "half savage" to touch his daughter. Charles had spent two years with the Algonquin Indians in Canada, and people hereabouts still seemed to mistrust him. But the pastor made no objection.

"Good morning. Miss Abigail Jewett, is it not?"

Abby giggled. "Aye, sir."

"Would you permit me to lug you to the garrison?" Charles stood and let his pack fall to the snow. "I'll leave my catch here until I return, and you can ride on my back." He crouched beside her.

Jane helped Abby climb onto his back and wrap her arms around his neck. "Hang on tight." Then she adjusted the knitted scarf over Abby's ears and wrapped the ends around her face.

"Hurry," Abby said as Charles stood. "It's cold."

Her father barked a laugh but said no more.

"Thank you, sir," Jane murmured.

Charles nodded at her, and she fancied his eyes twinkled, but perhaps they only reflected the starlight.

The men set off with long strides. John trotted behind them.

Jane stood for only a moment in the cutting wind, watching the tall shadows grow faint. An icy gust enveloped her, and she turned her back to it. As quickly as she could, she plodded back to the Jewetts' little home near the meetinghouse.

Christine met Jane at the door, breathless. "You're back so soon!"

Jane pulled off her shawl. "Charles Gardner met us and offered to help the Reverend Jewett with the children."

"Is Goody Baldwin on her way?" Christine asked.

"Not yet. I'm sure she'll come ere long."

Christine sighed and glanced toward the pallet in the corner where Goody Jewett lay. "I admit I was frightened to be here alone with her. In fact, I nearly ran across the way to see if Goody Deane could come. I've nursed women before, but not for this."

Jane smiled. Christine's nursing had no doubt been performed in the convent in Quebec City. The young woman had lived among the nuns for five years after her Indian captors sold her to the French.

"We shall be fine until the midwife gets here." Jane hung her wraps on a peg by the door and hurried to Elizabeth Jewett's bedside. "How are you?"

Goody Jewett smiled with clenched teeth. "Not so bad, but I expect I shall bleat and shout a bit soon. At least the children are not within hearing."

Jane smoothed the dark hair back from Elizabeth's forehead. "Christine and I shan't mind. We'll do whatever we can to help you."

Elizabeth caught her breath and braced against pain.

Jane eased down onto the edge of the featherbed and held her hand. Her only experience in midwifery was when her own child was born in an isolated farmhouse in Quebec. Although the villagers here in Cochecho knew she had been married to a French trapper, Jane had told no one in New Hampshire about her tiny, stillborn baby boy.

She could barely remember the things the neighbor woman in Quebec had done during the birth. Probably they wouldn't serve now, anyway. Jane's baby had been born too soon, and likely her labor was different from a normal, healthy childbirth. But she couldn't say any of that to Goody Jewett. She could only smile in sympathy and mop her brow with cool water while Christine brought fresh linens and kept the big kettle boiling.

She wished her friend Sarah Dudley were present. Sarah had recently married Richard Dudley, the young man she'd loved since childhood. Jane was sure that Sarah would know more about midwifery than she did.

A knock at the cottage door brought a surge of relief to Jane's heart.

Christine leaped up and admitted Captain Baldwin's wife and Ben.

"Well, so the babe is coming at last," the midwife said, bustling in and setting a basket on the floor.

"Aye, we thought to see this event a fortnight ago," Christine told her.

"Well, wee ones know their own best time."

When Goody Baldwin had warmed herself by the fire, Jane gladly gave place to her. The sun was up, and Christine allowed thirteen-year-old Ben Jewett only a few scant minutes to stand by the hearth. She passed him a biscuit and told him to go to the Heards', where all the children would stay until the baby had arrived and the arduous cleaning that would follow was completed.

Only minutes after Ben had left, his father returned, but Goody Baldwin instructed Jane to turn him away, as Goody Jewett's labor had progressed and a man was not wanted in the flurry of activity.

As the moment drew near, Christine retreated to their hostess's chair in a corner, her face pale. She sat still, with her eyes closed and her lips moving silently.

Jane wished she could also retreat to pray, but she knew her help was needed. Goody Baldwin kept her running for linen, water, string, a knife. . . . Jane was too busy to think about her own experience two years ago.

Suddenly it was over, and the baby was there in the midwife's hands. His first breath was a thin, broken wail.

Christine leaped to her feet and came to the bedside, staring down in wonder at the writhing, red little scrap of a boy. Before Jane even thought about calling his father, the door flew open, admitting the Reverend Jewett and a blast of icy wind.

"Well?" His pale face, lined with worry, and his intent dark eyes showed between his icy beard and his woolen hat.

"A fine little fellow you have, sir," said Goody Baldwin.

Pastor Jewett exhaled. "Praise God." He laughed and stepped forward to look at his third son.

"Not yet!" The midwife stood between him and the pallet. "Let us wash him up before you hold him."

Jane stepped forward. "Here, Pastor. You're freezing. Let me take your coat, and you sit near the fire for a few minutes. Melt the icicles out of your beard. When you've warmed up, you can hold the babe and visit with your wife."

The big man meekly obeyed her instructions, looking anxiously toward the bed as he peeled off his coat and handed it to Jane.

Charles Gardner at last reached his cottage and stomped the snow off his boots outside the door. He hurried to the fireplace. The coals he had banked several hours earlier glowed only faintly. He stirred them and stripped off his mittens so he could break pine cones and bits of kindling into smaller pieces with his chilled hands. A few minutes' care and soft blowing on the tinder rewarded him. The blaze sprang up, and he held out his aching hands to receive its warmth.

Assisting the Reverend Jewett had kept him out in the frigid air an extra hour, but Charles couldn't help being glad he'd had the opportunity. Jane Miller, though she might be strong, could not plod through the snow as quickly as he and the pastor. By sending her back to the parsonage, he'd helped not only the Jewett family but Jane herself. He was glad to know she was warm and safe.

He'd first noticed her eight months ago, when the governor of New Hampshire commissioned him, Captain Baldwin, and two other men to go to Quebec and redeem as many captives as they could from the French. Though she'd been married in Canada to a French farmer, she'd also been widowed there. Captain Baldwin had negotiated long hours with the authorities for her return.

In the end, Jane Robataille had agreed to give up any claim to her late husband's estate in Quebec, preferring to return to the English colonies. She had no family here in Cochecho; that much he knew. He seemed to recall that she'd been close to fulfilling a period of indenture when she was captured during the massacre more than five years ago. She'd reverted to her maiden name, Miller, and stayed at the Jewetts' house since her return last May.

Charles's respect for the parson had grown when the Jewett family took in not just Jane but two other returned captive women without homes. Some others in the town shunned the redeemed captives, a disheartening attitude Charles had experienced when he returned from his own stint with the Algonquin.

But the mood seemed to be changing in

the village. Sarah Minton, one of Jane's orphaned companions in the Jewett household, had married Richard Dudley just two months ago. The Dudleys were close neighbors of Charles, and he and Richard had been good friends for years. The newlyweds seemed to be accepted in the community, and Charles had heard no disparaging remarks about Sarah in months.

But Jane's marriage to the French voyageur — which he suspected had been performed against her will — put her in another category in the dour colonists' minds.

Of course, the third young woman at the Jewetts', Christine Hardin, was in even worse straits. She'd spent years in a nunnery in Quebec. No good Protestant wanted to associate with her, though the Jewetts treated her like a member of the family. She attended meeting every Sunday and seemed to listen intently to Pastor Jewett's sermons. Charles doubted she had renounced her Protestant faith, but that wouldn't matter to some people.

As the room warmed, Charles removed his coat and hung it on a peg, not too close to the fire. It soon began to drip, and the steam filled the cabin with the strong smell of wet wool.

He opened his pack and pulled out the carcasses he'd gathered before dawn — a beaver, two muskrats, and a mink. Too cold to skin them outside. His hands would freeze in minutes without gloves.

If his mother were alive, he'd have thrown them outside and waited to skin them later. But no women resided in the Gardner cabin now to chide him for making a mess of their floors.

He pulled his razor-sharp skinning knife from its sheath and set to work on the little mink first. The silky fur was so gentle on his calloused hands that he could barely feel it. Just the thing for a fine lady's winter bonnet and muff.

Jane Miller's face once more flashed through his consciousness. She would look lovely in furs and velvet. But a poor girl like Jane, a former indentured servant and captive, would likely never know such luxury. These furs would go on a ship to England in the spring, for some rich man to buy.

A firm rap on the door startled him, and he jumped, nicking his finger with the blade. He sighed at his own clumsiness.

"Ho, Charlie? Are you there?"

"Come in, Richard."

The door opened, and his friend came in, stamping his feet and shedding snow that lay unmelted near the door at the cold end of the room.

"Come and warm yourself," Charles said, concentrating on his job. "You're out early."

"Not as early as you, evidently."

"Aye, I had a good catch this morn."

"I came to see if you want to cut wood tomorrow."

"If it's warmer."

Richard nodded. "Not today, surely. But I need to finish cutting next year's firewood for Sarah and me, and for my folks, too."

"Aye. We'll trade work until it's done for us all." The skin of the little mink came free, and Charles set it aside.

"Sarah would never let me skin my catch in the house."

"Sarah doesn't live here." Charles tossed the tiny carcass into the fire.

Richard frowned at him and looked around. "You need a wife, Charlie."

"Ha! You're just saying that because you're still in the euphoric mist of new marriage."

"Yes, I am."

Charles laughed and pulled the large beaver onto the hearth before him. "Would you and your lady like a nice beaver tail for your supper?"

"Thank you, I'm sure Sarah would be delighted."

Charles severed the tail and set it to one side.

"I saw your eyes rest upon Jane Miller after the Sunday meeting. Of course, I wouldn't know, but my wife says Jane is looking rather pretty these days."

"Please, Richard." Charles slit the beaver's skin neatly up the belly, where the hide was thinnest. "I'm glad that you are happy, but I don't care to pursue the topic of marriage while I skin the bounty of my trapline."

Richard snorted a laugh. "You know you admire her."

"I do. I've told you so, and I make no secret of it. She's tough, she's deft with a needle, and she doesn't complain."

"And comely?"

Charles shrugged. "I couldn't say."

"Certainly you could."

"Not to you. It would be all over the village ere nightfall."

Richard's chuckle annoyed Charles. His friend had been married only two months, but already he thought himself an expert.

"You're worse than an old woman, Richard. Really. I never saw such a matchmaker."

Richard stooped and fed two small logs into the fire. "I went to the ordinary yesterday, and I heard a couple of young, unmarried men discussing Miss Miller in a favorable light."

Charles worked on in silence for a moment, but he couldn't keep still. "Who were they?"

"Oh, I can't tell you that. Every time you met them, your jealousy would rear up and make you dislike them. Can't have you being rude to decent fellows. Next thing, you'd be brawling."

"You're daft."

"Nay. I've no doubt one of them will seek to court her soon."

"It's none of my affair." But Charles wondered if perhaps he ought to approach the parson before one of the others did. Jane couldn't be much beyond twenty years of age. Though she had come to the village in May thin and bedraggled, she had gained flesh in the past few months, and she seemed to grow prettier as the weeks went by. He knew Richard was right. Several young men — and some not so young — watched Jane at Sunday meeting.

Richard glanced around once more. "You can't bring a wife to this sorry little cabin, though."

Charles bit his lower lip and concentrated on relieving the fat beaver of its fur. His father's plans to enlarge the little cabin into a fine farmhouse had come to nothing. John Gardner had died suddenly while his son was only half grown, and his widow was killed in the massacre, when Charles was taken captive.

"I can't complain about this farm," Charles said. "The town elders allowed me to inherit my father's land when I returned from Canada. Last year they admitted me as a freeman to the town's rolls. They didn't have to."

"Aye." Richard took another stick of firewood from the pile and tapped the edge of his boot with it. "It takes time to regain your losses when you've been away, especially the way you were. You're lucky this land wasn't given to someone else."

"It would have been if people weren't so frightened of Indian raids," Charles admitted. "But single-handed, I can never clear enough land to make this farm prosper. I have to fight the forest for every inch of ground I want to plant."

"I know. It's the same with us."

"But you have your father, and now Stephen is back."

Richard pressed his lips together and nodded. "True. My brother has been a help since he came back two months ago. But he's restless."

26

Charles looked up into his friend's eyes. "Do you think he won't stay?"

"I don't know." Richard leaned against the stone mantel. "I hope he will. Mother would be crushed if he left again."

Charles nodded. The same longing used to seize him. He'd think about leaving Cochecho and disappearing into the forest, walking northward and disappearing once more from the frontier community. But he'd left the savage life of the Algonquin. He'd gained his captors' trust and escaped from them of his own free will. If he thought about it long enough, he always put away those stray thoughts of returning to the wild life. Something kept him here. This land, this farm, these fellow Englishmen around him. But he wanted more.

He thought of Jane again. She didn't mingle much with the villagers, but he'd seen her laughing with the Jewett children and Sarah Dudley. Her pert nose and reddish-blond hair set off her solemn gray eyes. He always thought Jane looked like someone who had many interesting thoughts but kept them private. How he would like to hear them.

"Well, if I ever think of marrying, I'll have to build up this farm. I couldn't support a family the way it is."

"Yes, you ought to have a cow or at least a goat."

"And a dog to warn me if any Indians come skulking around?"

Richard laughed. "I think your knowledge of the brutes and their language protects you better than a dog could."

Charles resumed his work. "How about making us a little breakfast, Richard?"

Richard straightened and glanced toward the door. "I should get home. Sarah will have breakfast ready and wonder where I am. But I'll bring in some more wood for you and put some samp on, if you like." He turned to the shelf where Charles kept his foodstuffs and opened the crock of parched corn.

"Don't bother," Charles said. "I've got some Indian pudding left over from last night's supper in the kettle yonder."

"All right, then, I'll leave you." Richard settled his hat over his ears and pulled on his mittens. "Come by in the morning with your ax if it's warmer. You can breakfast with us, and we'll go into the woods together."

"Aye."

When his friend had left, Charles finished his task with painstaking care. He stretched the skins and hung them on the cabin wall

28

outside then cleaned up the floor and the hearth. Finally, he brought in a bucket of snow to melt so that he could wash the blood from his hands. The cut on his finger stung, but it didn't seem to go deep.

A well was another thing on his list of improvements to make. In summer he hauled water all the way from the river. In winter he melted snow. He must dig a well come spring. Richard and his brother, Stephen, would help, if Stephen stayed in the colony. Then Charles would have water at his doorstep, like the Dudley family did inside their stockade.

That was another thing. Should he fence his dwelling? Would it really make him safer? Charles doubted it. Richard was probably right about that. Charles's own experience with the Indians probably protected him better than a dog or a stockade would. But a woman might feel safer with those amenities.

Once more he thought of Jane Miller. She'd been through tough times, but on the long march back from Quebec, he'd never once heard her complain. She knew how to work hard. But was she ready to marry again?

Two

The Reverend Jewett went to bring the five older children home from the Heards' garrison the next day. Jane dressed the new baby in fresh clothes while Christine helped Goody Jewett wash and change into her clean shift. Tears sprang into Jane's eyes at the thought of the little boy she had lost, but memories couldn't dim her delight for the Jewett family.

When the children entered, they all rushed to the pallet in the corner of the room. Constance and Abby snuggled up on each side of their mother and gazed adoringly at their new brother. John stared for a long moment at the little one, but Ben only gave the baby a glance and went to the hearth for the water bucket. He picked it up and went out the door without a word.

"What shall we name him?" Goody Jewett asked the other children as they crowded around. Her husband plopped Ruth on the coverlet beside Abby and pulled a chair over to the bedside. Ben brought in a bucketful of snow and dumped it into the large kettle on the hearth then went to stand behind his father's chair.

"Let's call him Samuel," said John.

"That's Papa's name," Abby objected.

"So?" John scowled at her.

"We can't have two Samuels."

Both parents laughed, and the pastor said gently, "Some families do, Abby. But what would you suggest, John?"

"David?" the boy asked.

"I know," Constance cried. "Goliath."

Everyone laughed. During the family's time of devotions two nights past, her father had read the story of David and Goliath.

Jane loved watching the family together. The Jewetts epitomized the dream she'd had for many years. Some parents seemed reluctant to love their children, as many died early in life. But in spite of having lost two babies and feeling the cruel pain of grief, Samuel and Elizabeth Jewett never stinted their youngsters of affection.

When she was younger, Jane had longed for a loving family of her own. But her unfortunate marriage in Quebec had failed to bring her anything resembling the happiness she saw here.

Jane knew she couldn't stay here at the parsonage forever. The little house was growing more and more crowded. The nameless infant made ten in all. Jane and Christine shared the small loft with the three Jewett girls, while the parents and the two boys slept in the main room. Although Goody Jewett needed their help for now, Jane couldn't help feeling the parson's family would be better off if she or Christine left. Since neither of them wished to marry, Jane often thought one of them should hire out to another household.

After supper, the pastor stood and came to the hearth. "Let me pour that hot water into the dishpan for you."

"I can do it, sir."

"Nay, let me."

She stood back and watched him deftly swing the crane, bringing the simmering kettle of water off the fire.

"It's difficult to get a private word in this house, but I should like such with you," the pastor murmured.

Jane stared at him in surprise. "Indeed, sir?"

"Aye." He glanced about at the others. Christine was stacking the dishes at the table, and the other children had once more gathered about their mother. "A man approached me at the meetinghouse this afternoon as I was practicing my sermon. He mentioned your name."

"Mine?"

"Yours, Miss Miller. He asked if my wife and I would accept callers on your behalf. I told him that would be your decision."

Jane inhaled, feeling a sharp anxiety pricking at her lungs. "Well, sir, I . . ."

"You needn't see him if you don't wish to."

"Thank you." She knotted her apron between her restless hands. "Rather than marrying, I've thought of trying to find a place where I could work, though I have no wish to leave here in a hurry. Especially if your wife has need of me."

"Elizabeth is delighted to have your help and Christine's at this time," he assured her.

"Might I know who be asking, sir?"

He nodded. "It's Lemuel Given."

Jane frowned. "I cannot picture him."

"He's a widower. Lives on Dover Point."

"A sailor, then?"

"A fisherman," Pastor Jewett said. "He has five children. I expect he needs someone to take charge while he's at sea."

A rush of panic caused her stomach to lurch. She would be thrown into a strange family and expected to bring order while the head of the household was away. She recalled the long months in Canada while her husband went off to trade and the many trials she had endured alone. Was she ready to keep house for another man who was absent much of the time? Could she welcome him home at intervals and pretend gladness to see a man she hardly knew? What if he were cruel and she couldn't like him? What if the children were spoiled and rebellious? What if he despised her and treated her like a servant?

She looked up into the pastor's gentle face. "He's not looking for temporary help, is he?"

"Nay, Jane. He wants a wife."

"Ah." She sighed. "I do not wish to marry at this time, but if you think it expedient . . ."

"Far from it." He smiled. "You are welcome here for as long as you wish. You and Christine both. My wife and I are glad you consider this your home."

"Thank you," she whispered. "Then I shall decline."

She turned away and began to scrub the dishes. Could she really stay in this cramped, noisy cottage much longer? The parson seemed sincere in telling her that she could remain without arousing resentment. Did she still hope for a home of her own? She'd had that and found no joy in it. But was that home really hers? She'd worked from morning to night for Monsieur Robataille, and after his death she'd been forced to give up the farm.

No, that wasn't the dream she'd cherished as a girl. Even though she'd been wrenched from her own family and thrust into servitude at the age of eleven, and then captured by savages a few years later, she'd always assumed that one day she would marry a man of her choosing. A young man, her age or close to it. One she admired and perhaps even loved. They would work together and form a family and a homestead they could be proud of.

Jane realized that she had never given up that dream.

After the sermon on Sunday, Charles waited at the back of the meetinghouse for Richard and Sarah to come down the aisle. In summer he'd have waited outside, but the temperatures, though somewhat moderated from the previous week, were still uncomfortable if one stood about for long in the open.

Sarah paused to talk to the Jewett children and Jane Miller. Charles assumed Christine

Hardin had stayed at the parsonage with Goody Jewett and the new babe. Jane's face was more animated than usual as she and the children talked to Sarah. Even across the room, he could tell by their facial expressions and gestures that they were describing the baby. Richard moved on toward him, leaving his wife with her friends.

Jane seemed to be measuring the infant's length with her slender, delicate hands, and Sarah's smile brought an answering glint to Jane's eyes.

She's beautiful! Charles forced himself to look away lest anyone else witness his fascination.

"I believe you're smitten," Richard said at his side.

Too late. In spite of the chilly room, Charles felt heat flush his face beneath the cover of his beard.

"And I believe you're impertinent." He turned to face Richard squarely. "All right, I agree with what you said the other day. She would make a good wife. Do we have to talk about this here?" Charles glanced around to see if anyone else had heard his comment.

Richard leaned toward him and lowered his voice. "You'd best act soon if you intend to. I heard Lemuel Given telling Obed Bates earlier that he asked permission of the parson to call on Miss Miller."

Charles's heart sank. "Oh? What came of it? Are the banns to be read soon?"

"Nay." Richard chuckled. "Apparently he approached the reverend several days ago but only received his reply last evening. It was not to Given's liking."

Charles smiled. "The parson told him to stay away from her?"

"Given says the reverend told him she's not ready to remarry. But I also heard a whisper from another saying Miss Miller begged the Jewetts not to make her receive Given's addresses. She thinks him old and overly blessed with brats."

"She didn't say that!" Charles stared at him in dismay.

"I doubt she did, but you know the gossips in this town. They'll take what one man tells and twist it into something totally foreign. But I heard Given himself say that she thinks she's too good for an English farmer, now that she's been once wedded to a Frenchman."

Charles frowned at him in confusion. "Why would anyone consider marrying an Englishman a step downward?"

"Well, if the Englishman were Lemuel

Given . . ." Richard's crooked smile brought Charles around to seeing the humorous side of the tale.

"Right." Charles looked over at the Jewett family again.

Sarah was still talking to Jane and had twined six-year-old Abby's hand in hers. Jane held the toddler, Ruth, and Constance clutched a fold of Jane's skirt, watching with large, round eyes as the two young women talked.

"Does Sarah miss living in the Jewetts' household?"

"Some," Richard said. "But she's going round to see the new babe and visit Goody Jewett tomorrow if the weather holds. She tells me the parsonage is a haven of blissful confusion, and she loves the family as if they were her own kin. But she prefers our quiet little nest now."

Charles smiled at his tall, rugged friend. He never would have believed Richard could become so besotted. "Your wife has made you mellow."

"You can be as contented." Richard gave him a meaningful grin. "Strike now, before some other hot-blooded young fellow asks for permission to court her."

"I thought you said she isn't ready to remarry."

"Not I." Richard nodded a return greeting to a couple filing toward the door of the meetinghouse. "The parson said that. Or rather, Given said that the parson said it. But he's twice her age and gone to sea fishing half the time. What's to become of her if she marries a man like that?"

"With all the youngsters at his house, she would probably become a drudge."

Richard nodded. "I suspect that when a charming young man with a good farm and no encumbrances comes around, Miss Miller will find that she is ready."

Charles didn't like to think Jane bided her time for an advantageous situation to come her way. Didn't character count . . . and feelings? Was love totally out of the question? On the other hand, why shouldn't a woman expect her husband to take care of her?

He looked toward the front of the room once more. The little group was breaking up. Jane was tying Ruth's bonnet under the little girl's chin, and Sarah hurried down the aisle toward Richard.

Richard leaned toward him and whispered a parting thought. "She's not skinny any longer, Charles. She's healthy and strong. Strike now."

■ ■ ■ ■

A few days later, the sun shone brightly on the settlement. Charles and Richard had finished putting up their firewood, and Charles walked to the village.

He found the Reverend Jewett huddled on one of the benches near a window in the bitterly cold meetinghouse.

"You're likely to freeze in here, sir."

The parson looked up from his open Bible. "Good day, Charles. I brought a warm soapstone with me" — he nudged a cloth-wrapped bundle with his stockinged foot — "but it seems to have lost its heat now."

"We ought to have built a hearth in here."

"Nay, folks bring their soapstones and rugs and warming pans of a Sunday. 'Twould take a prodigious amount of wood to heat this building."

Charles considered that and nodded. "In a way, sir, that's what I've come about. I wondered if you've plenty of wood for your house."

The parson cleared his throat and looked up at him. "Thank you for asking. We've enough for this winter, I suppose, if the weather doesn't turn icy again. I plan to cut some for next year soon. We've had so much going on at the house, with the new addition and all . . ."

"Yes, a fine little fellow, I hear."

"Well, he's not as sturdy as Ben and John were. Smallish child."

Charles nodded, wondering what constituted a smallish baby. "Well, sir, I'd enjoy helping you cut your firewood, if you'd like the company."

"Why, Charles, that's most good of you. Are you free later this week?" Jewett fumbled about with his feet until he found his shoes.

"Yes, sir."

The reverend closed his Bible, pulled the shoes on, and stood. "I should have this week's sermon ready by Friday. I could perhaps go into the woods with you that day, if the weather holds."

"That would be fine, sir."

"Will you take dinner with us now?" The parson picked up his soapstone bundle and moved toward the door, and Charles walked with him. "I come over here to study, even though it's cold. At home, with the children cooped up, there are just too many distractions. You understand."

Charles nodded. "I can well imagine."

"Yes, well, children underfoot and young

41

ladies at work. Don't mistake my meaning — they are a big help, Miss Hardin and Miss Miller. But when you put six children and three women in a small house, and the baby cries and the loom thumps and the boys start their horseplay —"

"That reminds me, sir." Charles grabbed the topic quickly before it could get away. "You mentioned the young ladies in your household."

The reverend paused with his hand on the door latch. "Yes?"

"I . . . well . . ." Charles couldn't hold his gaze. He pulled in a deep breath and rushed on. "I wondered if perhaps Miss Jane Miller would . . . would take callers of an evening, sir. If you think I'm not too bold."

The pastor ran his fingers through his beard and scratched his chin. "I don't know, Charles. I had another inquiry last week, and she told me she'd rather not. But he was an older man, in a different situation than yours. I can ask her if you'd like me to."

Charles gulped, and it felt as though he'd swallowed a brick. "If you wouldn't mind, sir."

Jewett eyed him thoughtfully. "She's made it clear to both my wife and me that she prefers the single state for now. You know she had a bad experience in Canada?"

"Aye, sir. That is, I know she was married briefly, and her husband met an untimely end."

"Yes. And I understand he was much older than she. Perhaps that accounts for her aversion to . . . the gentleman I mentioned. Well, I'll put a word in for you. We'd like to see Miss Miller well settled, with a steady man."

Charles's chest expanded. The pastor thought him steady. That was more than most of the villagers would give him. "You can tell me Friday what she says, sir, when we go to cut wood."

Jewett tucked his burdens under his arms and pulled on knit woolen mittens. "Oh, why don't you just come by this evening? If she is against it, she can tell you."

Charles hesitated. He hated the idea of receiving a lady's rebuff in person. "I suppose I could."

"All right, do that. Now come have some dinner. I'm sure eleven won't matter more than ten for the stew pot."

"Oh, thank you, sir, but I need to stop at the trader's and then get on home. But I'll stop by this evening."

They stepped out into the dazzling January sun reflected from the snow. Charles waved and hurried across the packed snow of the village street. He was hungry, but he couldn't bear the thought of sitting at table with her, knowing the pastor knew his heart but Jane did not. He'd blush and stammer like a girl.

But even if he declined the dinner invitation, there was no getting out of the pickle he'd put himself in now. Jane would decide his future. Either she would say no and he would continue in his sorry plight, single and independent, a bit lonesome, but also too embarrassed to meet her gaze ever again across the village green, or — dare he think it? — she might say yes, and his life would never be the same.

THREE

Jane stepped over Ruthie Jewett and carefully carried a cup of milk and a slice of rye bread to the toddler's mother, who was sitting in her chair. It was Elizabeth Jewett's favorite spot in the house — the only chair with a back. Her husband had labored many hours over it for her.

"What's this? Another supper?" Goody Jewett held up a hand in protest.

Jane smiled. "You need something extra to build your blood up, Goody Baldwin told me."

Christine paused in her sweeping of the hearth. "Aye. She said to feed you six times a day so you will regain your strength."

Elizabeth reached for the pewter cup. "You girls will spoil me, to be sure. Why, after Ben was born, I was up and doing all my kitchen work the next day."

"That were then, and this be now," Jane said firmly. "Drink all of that."

45

Goody Jewett meekly put the cup to her lips. A thin wail sounded from the low bed, and she stopped without drinking, looking toward the corner.

"You eat this morsel. I'll get the baby." Jane put the slice of bread in Elizabeth's hand and turned to pick up the infant. As she'd suspected, his clouts and gown were soaked. She took the small quilt he'd lain on, as well, and carried him over to the bench nearer the hearth, where they often changed him. The far reaches of the room were always cold, and she didn't want to chill the babe.

The little girls clustered around her. John and Ben stayed on their pallet on the other side of the room, where they were playing with a half dozen tiny wooden men their father had carved for them. The pastor was out calling on the sick, but a kettle of water steamed on the hearth so that he could have a cup of hot, brewed wintergreen leaves when he came home.

"Abby, would you fetch your brother a fresh gown?" Jane asked. Abigail scurried to the shelves near the bed to get one.

"There's a good girl," her mother said with a smile.

"I'm glad you named him Joseph," Jane told Goody Jewett as she untied the knot

46

that held the baby's layered clouts together.

"I like it," she replied. Christine continued sweeping, but her lips turned upward, and Goody Jewett asked, "What are you smiling at, Christine?"

Jane and the Jewett girls looked up with interest. Christine never intruded in a conversation, preferring silence, but Jane was sure she had plenty of thoughts whirling about in her head.

"I only thought how much better it is than Hezekiah, as the parson thought to name him," Christine said, dipping her head and digging into the corner by the wood box with her broom.

"Oh, Hezekiah," Elizabeth laughed. "I would have none of that. I don't think my husband was truly set on it, but suggested it to startle us ladies."

Christine stood the broom in the corner and untied her apron. "Come now, Constance, Abby. You, too, Ruth. It's time for you to get to bed. Gather up your things." She herded the three girls up the ladder to the loft. Ruth had lately been judged old enough to sleep up there, after the parson and Ben constructed a low railing across the front edge of the platform above the main room.

Jane deftly wrapped a small blanket about

the baby and placed him in his mother's open arms. "Now, Ben and John, you strong boys must help me bring in enough firewood for the night."

"The boys can do it," Elizabeth said.

"Nay, 'twill be sooner done if I help," Jane replied. She knew the boys would stay at their task better if an adult joined them. John found it all too easy to leave off his chores and begin building a snow fort.

She took her woolen cloak from its peg and threw it over her shoulders and then wrapped a shawl about her head. As she donned her mittens, she noted with satisfaction that the boys were putting on their coats and hats. They were good boys and usually obeyed her and Christine now as readily as they did their mother.

The three of them went out into the glittering dooryard. The three-quarter moon reflected in sparkles off the snow in eerie beauty.

"Three good armloads each will do it," Jane said. "Load me up, Ben."

She stood by the woodpile with her arms outstretched, and Ben stacked five medium sticks across them. John stepped up and imitated her posture, and Ben loaded him, too; then he began to choose his own burden.

Jane turned toward the doorstone, but the crunch of boots on the snow made her look toward the street. She expected to see the parson arriving home, but instead Charles Gardner's tall frame loomed in the moonlight.

"Good evening, sir," she said.

Charles stopped and stood for a moment uncertainly then glanced toward the door. "The parson said I might come calling."

"He's not home this eve. Goody Branwell be ill, and he also planned to visit Mr. Otis and check on his injury."

"Yes, I heard Mr. Otis cut his leg badly. But I didn't really come to see the reverend." Charles glanced toward the small window covered with oiled paper. A faint glow spoke of the warmth within, the candlelight and a fire on the hearth, the children's laughter, and the closeness of a large family. "He told me he would ask a certain young lady within his house if she would receive me as a caller."

His words startled Jane. Charles looked decidedly uncomfortable, shifting from one foot to another. A certain young lady? The only young lady within the house right now was Christine.

"Be you coming to call on Miss Christine?" Ben asked, joining them with his arms full of firewood.

Charles opened his mouth and darted a look toward Jane as though asking for help. Of course. He was embarrassed and needed some assistance.

"I'll tell her you're here." Jane spun to open the door. A pang of disappointment struck her, but that was silly. A young man actually had his eye on Christine. How wonderful for her friend. Of course, Christine wouldn't think it was wonderful. She always tried to stay as far away from men as she could.

Jane managed to raise the latch without spilling her load. She dropped her wood into the box by the hearth, noticing that Christine had not come down from the loft. Jane heard her low voice as she spoke to the three little girls she was tucking in for the night.

She went to the ladder and scrambled up it. Below her, John and Ben came in with their firewood. Charles entered behind them, closing the door firmly to shut out the cold night air.

"Good evening," Jane heard him say.

"Good evening to you, sir," Goody Jewett replied.

At the top of the ladder, Jane hesitated. Christine was kneeling on the edge of the pallet shared by Abby and Ruth, listening to Abby's bedtime prayer.

"And help Mr. Otis's leg to get better, please. Amen," the little girl said.

"Christine," Jane hissed.

Christine looked around at her, with inquiry widening her hazel eyes. Her mousy brown hair was held back with a dark ribbon, but after a long day's work, wisps escaped and hung haphazardly about her face. Jane wished her friend would take more notice of her appearance. Now, of all times, she wished Christine were beautiful. But Charles must have looked beyond the tall young woman's plain features and lackluster hair and seen Christine's inner beauty.

Below her, Jane heard the boys dump their loads of firewood, and the door opened and closed as they went out for more.

"There's a young man here to see you."

"What?" Christine's eyes opened even wider.

"Charles Gardner is down below. He wants to see you. Did the pastor tell you he was coming?"

"Nay." Christine edged forward on her knees, just far enough to see down into the great room below. She caught her breath and sprang back into the shadows. "Make

51

him go away."

Jane couldn't help smiling. She leaned forward and touched Christine's arm. "Surely wishing him a good evening would not be amiss."

"I can't. Please don't make me go down there." Christine's distaste seemed to border on fear as she shrank back beneath the eaves of the cottage. "Please, Jane. Tell him whatever you will, but I can't do it. You know I don't wish to marry. Ever."

"All right. I'm sorry I distressed you. But if you are certain —"

"I am."

Jane nodded slowly. "I'll tell him."

"Tell him graciously. I'm sure he's a nice young man. It's not him so much. It's just . . ." Christine bit her lip and looked away.

Jane noticed that Abby was watching them, bright-eyed, though the two younger girls had already drifted into sleep.

"You'll make him understand, won't you?" Christine pleaded.

"I shall do my best." Jane backed down the ladder, her knees trembling. What a dilemma she was in. From what Charles had let fall, she assumed the minister had agreed to speak to Christine, as he had to Jane when Lemuel Given approached him. But

Christine had obviously heard nothing about a potential suitor.

Perhaps Goody Jewett knew something of the circumstances. Her hostess was conversing easily with Charles Gardner, who was now seated on a bench near her. Jane couldn't help but notice his pleasant features, neatly trimmed beard, and glossy dark hair. It was too bad Christine wouldn't give him a hearing.

Ben and John brought in more wood, and Ben joined Charles and his mother. "Sir, could you show me sometime how to set a fox trap? Father found a den at the end of our garden last fall, and we see them now and again. I want to catch them."

Jane sidled up to Goody Jewett, who held the new baby in her arms. "Would you like me to lay Joseph on the bed?"

"Nay, we're fine. Sit down by the hearth with Goodman Gardner."

"I?" Jane stared at her.

"He's come to call on you, not on Ben and me."

Jane turned just enough to see whether Charles was still talking to Ben. He threw a glance her way and stood when their gaze met. She leaned closer to Elizabeth and whispered, "I beg your pardon, ma'am. I thought he came to call on Christine."

Elizabeth stared back for a moment then glanced at Charles with a brief smile. "Won't you be seated again, Goodman Gardner?" To Jane she whispered, "Did not my husband tell you?"

Jane felt a large lump rise in her throat. "Nay."

Elizabeth's smile seemed frozen on her face. After a long moment, she gave a nervous laugh. "Well, this is awkward. Goodman Gardner, please excuse our confusion. My husband told me of your conversation with him, but it seems neither of us mentioned it to Miss Miller. And she seems to suffer the illusion that you are calling on our other guest, Miss Hardin."

"Forgive me," Charles said, turning his hat about in his hands. "I failed to make my meaning clear outside, and I feared there was a misunderstanding. I hope no one is discomfited." His gaze swept the edge of the loft for an instant.

There was no sign of Christine above them, but Jane thought how relieved she must be, if she were listening. And how did she feel herself? She felt the blood rush to her cheeks.

Charles himself looked very uncomfortable. He gave a little shrug and attempted a smile that was only partly successful. "The reverend did tell me to just stop in tonight. Perhaps he thought we needed no intermediary. He said you would tell me if you objected to my presence."

He waited, and Jane could not quite meet his gaze.

"My dear, why don't you make some wintergreen tea for our guest?" Elizabeth asked. She turned to her boys. "John, you must get to bed. Ben, if you wish to read from Mr. Bunyan's book for a while, you may, but you must take the candle over near your bed."

The boys said good night to Charles.

Jane seized Elizabeth's suggestion and took the steaming kettle from the fire. She poured its contents into the teapot that she had earlier set out in preparation for the parson's refreshment then started toward the door with the empty kettle.

"May I help you?" Charles was suddenly beside her, and she jumped.

"I was only going to get more snow to melt for the pastor's tea when he returns."

"Allow me to fetch it."

Charles took the kettle from her hand and went out the door.

Jane turned at once to Elizabeth. "Goody Jewett, what am I to do?"

Elizabeth eyed her with some surprise.

"Whatever do you mean, child? Be a courteous hostess."

"But I told your husband only days ago that I did not wish to receive gentlemen callers."

"Oh." The baby fussed, and Elizabeth lifted him to rest against her shoulder. "Does that apply to Charles Gardner, as well?"

"I . . ." The panic eased somewhat as Jane met Elizabeth's steady gaze.

"He's a nice young man and a diligent worker. Why not make him welcome and converse with him?" Elizabeth patted little Joseph's back, but he began to wail softly in spite of her attention. "It would only be fair to get acquainted with him a bit before you decide whether you wish to know him better."

"But if I let him stay and then decide to turn him away, it will be awful for him. And people will talk."

"People in this village will talk anyway," Elizabeth agreed. "Here, help me move my chair yonder so I can feed this babe."

The door opened as Jane helped her settle in at the other end of the room with the baby. Charles brought in the kettle full of snow and hung it over the coals.

"Shall I build up your fire, ma'am?"

he asked.

"Yes, thank you," Elizabeth said. "It's getting chilly in here."

He worked at the hearth for a minute with his back to them.

Jane wondered if he were as embarrassed as she felt. She went to the cupboard and took down two pewter mugs. "Would you like tea, ma'am?" she asked Elizabeth.

"No, thank you. I'll wait until my husband returns and have a cup with him."

Charles stood and brushed the bark off his hands. "Shall I bring in more firewood? Or if you've buckets, I could get you water so you wouldn't have to haul it in the morning."

"We've ample now," Jane said.

Charles hesitated, looking from her to Goody Jewett across the room and back. "I . . . don't need to stay if you'd rather I didn't, Miss Miller."

She felt her color deepen. "Nay, it was kind of you to call, sir. Won't you be seated?" She carried the cups over, and they both sat stiffly on the bench holding their tea and staring into the fire.

Charles cleared his throat. "Captain Baldwin said last spring that you dwelt at Dover Point before . . . before you were taken by the Pennacook."

"Aye," Jane said, grateful the silence was broken.

"Were your people killed in the massacre? I thought most of the destruction was here at Cochecho."

She nodded. "My parents died nearly twelve years ago. I was destitute, and though I was young, my uncle indentured me to a family needing domestic help."

Charles nodded, obviously wanting her to go on.

"My master had come to Cochecho to do business with Major Waldron." Jane caught her breath as the memories of that awful night returned. It was only by chance that she and the couple for whom she worked were at the major's garrison when the massacre occurred. Her hand shook so that she thought she might spill her hot tea. She steadied the cup with her other hand and raised it carefully to her lips, taking just a tiny sip of the scalding liquid.

"It was a dreadful night," Charles said.

"Yes," she whispered.

"What were your duties for your employer?"

Jane sighed. "I served the lady and worked in the kitchen. They had another girl, Betty, working for them, as well, and she tended the children. But toward the last, when I

58

was older, sometimes I watched them, too. When the master decided to bring his wife here with him to see the major, they left the young ones home with Betty. It was only to be a three-day journey, and they brought me to wait on the mistress. By chance, they arrived here the night the savages struck."

Elizabeth Jewett stirred. "You never told me that, my dear. I knew you were orphaned, but not that you were bound."

"My term of indenture was nearly over."

"How long was it?"

"Seven years. I had only one year left."

"That's a long time to serve another person," Charles said.

"Aye." Jane stood and walked across the cabin. It had seemed forever when she was told, at the age of eleven, that for seven years she belonged to Mr. Plaisted. She did not wish to recall those bleak and lonely years. "Is Joseph sleeping again?"

"Yes," said Elizabeth. "I think he'll rest now. If you'll just lay him down and put the coverlet over him . . ."

A stamping and bustle outside the door warned them of the pastor's return.

With the baby in her arms, Jane quickly flipped the edge of the blanket over Joseph's head to keep him from being chilled by the blast of cold air that entered with his father.

The moment he saw Charles, the Reverend Jewett burst out with a hearty greeting. "Well, Charles! I forgot you were coming. Welcome. I trust my wife and Miss Miller have made you comfortable."

"Hush, sir," Elizabeth warned him gently, a finger to her lips.

The baby wriggled, but Jane rocked him gently and held him close until he settled down again. His warm little body nestled against her, and she gazed down at the pink face, so sweet in repose.

Pastor Jewett hung up his wraps and went to sit with Charles. He launched into an account of his ailing parishioners' conditions.

Jane laid the baby on the bed after a few minutes and fixed tea for the pastor and his wife. Ben had blown out his candle and settled down next to John to sleep, and the four adults conversed in low tones for another half hour.

After the two men had confirmed their plan to cut wood together on Friday, Charles rose.

"Must you leave so soon?" the pastor asked.

"Aye, sir. It's late, and I must run my trapline early."

Jane sprang up and brought the coat Charles had earlier hung near the door.

"Come back again any evening," his host said. "I am usually at home, unless some ill folk need me."

"I should like to." Charles glanced at Jane and raised his eyebrows in question.

She realized he was asking her permission to call again. She was still a bit annoyed that the pastor had arranged this evening without consulting her. Still, it hadn't turned out so badly. She swallowed hard and managed to get out, "Please do, sir."

Elizabeth smiled in approval, and Charles gave her a nod that Jane construed as favorable.

A moment later he was gone, and Jane hurried about, putting away the tea tin and rinsing out the mugs.

"Mr. Jewett, I must tell you that you've been remiss," Elizabeth said to her husband.

He eyed her archly. "In what way, my dear?"

"You failed to tell Jane that young Goodman Gardner planned to call, and it set her all aflutter."

"Dear me, was I supposed to tell her? Forgive me, ladies. I trust his company was not too excruciating?"

Jane flushed, recalling her mistake. "I thought —"

Elizabeth laughed. "Jane is just fine, but

I'm afraid poor Christine was a bit frightened."

"How so?" the parson asked.

"Why, Jane told her Charles Gardner was here to call on her, and Christine would have none of it."

Jane faced the couple squarely and straightened her shoulders. "It was all my fault, sir. I mistook his meaning when he told me and Ben he'd come to call on a certain young lady in the house. We were outside, you see, and Christine was the only eligible young lady within at the moment. I'm afraid I rather botched things."

Elizabeth chuckled. "I'll talk to Christine on the morrow. She must be quite pleased that he came to see you, not her, Jane."

The reverend nodded. "It did my heart good to see you treating him well. Charles is a steady lad. I do hope I didn't cause you any distress by telling him he might call and ask your opinion of the matter. My intention was only to let you make your own decision."

"Perhaps it was for the best, sir," Jane said, not quite looking at him. Though she didn't wish to say so, she had found Charles Gardner's company to be tolerable. Of course, that didn't mean she was ready to get married again.

"Ah, yes," said the pastor. "If I'd fore-warned you, you might have turned him away without a chance to learn his charms."

"Now, Samuel," Elizabeth scolded. "See how red Jane's cheeks are. You mustn't tease her so."

Jane was tempted to rebuke the parson herself but thought better of it. His wife handled the job creditably on her own.

She headed for the ladder and nodded to them both. "Good night, ma'am, sir."

FOUR

After a week of warm weather in mid-January, the snow shrank and patches of dry grass were laid bare on the village green. Jane packed her mending in a basket one clear day and persuaded Ben Jewett to accompany her in walking the mile to Richard and Sarah Dudley's new home.

Richard's house squatted beside the trail within shouting distance of his father's stockaded home, with only one cornfield between it and the forest. Jane still felt the ominous gloom of the vast woodland whenever she ventured out of the village. Strong memories of the massacre still assailed her. The weeks she had spent on the arduous trail north with the Pennacook Indians remained vivid in her mind. She and Ben quickened their steps without speaking of the past.

"I'm so glad you came!" Sarah took Jane's cloak and shawl and hung them on a peg as

Ben hurried back toward home. "Tell me all that is going on at the parsonage. Is the baby well? Is Goody Jewett regaining her strength?"

"Yes, both are gaining." Jane looked around at the neat little room and inhaled the spicy scent of baking and dried fruit. Richard had built the cabin with a kitchen and a larger sitting room below and two rooms above, one on each side of the central chimney. "You have a fine home."

"Thank you. All the men of the village helped raise it for us, you know. Richard's father and Charles Gardner came every day for weeks to do the finish work. Sit here near the fire, Jane, and I'll fix us a biscuit and a cup of sweet cider."

Jane sat down on the settle and unpacked her mending, which consisted largely of the Jewett children's socks with holes worn in the toes and heels. "I brought extra darning floss in case you needed some."

"Oh, thank you. I do go through a prodigious amount, keeping Richard's socks in repair." Sarah fixed their refreshment and brought it over. She set the cups and a plate with two buttered biscuits on a stool within easy reach.

"You've butter in January. Hasn't your cow gone dry?" Jane felt hungry just seeing the fluffy white biscuits split and spread with yellow butter.

"Goody Dudley packed away several crocks last summer and fall in her spring-house. I don't expect it will last both house-holds all winter, but we're enjoying it."

Jane accepted her offer of the plate and chose half a biscuit. She wasted no time sinking her teeth into it. "Mmm. I don't believe the Jewetts have had butter since before you left us."

"Well, you shall take some home with you." Sarah brought over a basket of raw wool and her wool cards and sat down near Jane. "I shall sit with you a few minutes before I begin to get dinner."

"I shall help you when the time comes," Jane assured her.

Sarah laughed. "It's nothing to get dinner for you, Richard, and myself after cooking at the Jewetts' for months."

"Never quite enough for all those hungry children," Jane agreed.

"And before that, in the Indian village, we never had much to work with. Corn, beans, squash, venison, fish. Times of plenty at harvest or when a hunting party returned, but mostly short rations for all, especially in winter." Sarah shook her head and looked about.

Jane noticed the strings of dried apples and slabs of pumpkin hanging from the rafters with bunches of onions and herbs. Several crocks and casks of meal, flour, molasses, and pickled meat and vegetables, along with sacks of salt and sugar, filled the shelves or stood about the edge of the kitchen floor.

Sarah continued, "We are blessed with abundance here. What I could not provide myself this fall, Mother Dudley gave me — cheese, bacon, preserves. Richard and I live very well. I'm afraid I'll soon be fat."

Jane laughed. "You look contented, indeed. I'm happy that you are so well fixed. But I know you didn't marry him for his pantry."

"That's true. And I've been trying to fatten his brother and Charles Gardner. Those two young men are still far too thin. Of course, Charles has not come round much of late."

Jane realized Sarah was watching her closely, and she studiously tended to her darning weave on one of John Jewett's stockings.

But Sarah was not about to drop the subject. "Charles tells Richard he's been spending two evenings a week at the parsonage."

"Indeed." Jane reached the end of her thread, knotted it, and snipped it carefully off. "It is true."

"Richard is of the opinion that he will marry soon."

Jane felt her cheeks flush. "Is he?"

"Of course we should love to see him settled," Sarah went on. "He's such a dear friend to Richard. And having you as a neighbor would be — Oh, Jane, I'm delighted for you both."

"Don't be premature, Sarah. He's only come and sat by the fireside for three evenings to date. That does not make a marriage."

"I expect all the village folk think it will, though."

Jane smiled. "Well, I admit I like him better than I thought I would."

"Charles is a good man," Sarah said.

"I'm sure of it. It's just . . . I wasn't thinking of marrying again. Not yet, anyway. But now it seems I will have to make a decision."

Sarah eyed her soberly. "You and Charles have many things in common. You've both lost your own families, and you were both taken by the Indians during the massacre."

"Yes, though when we were abducted, we were put in separate bands. I don't remem-

68

ber meeting Charles until he and Captain Baldwin redeemed me from the French. But we both made that grim journey, it's true, and we've both experienced shunning when we returned, as did you." Jane couldn't keep a tinge of bitterness from her voice.

Sarah reached over and squeezed her hand. "So many people have been in captivity and lived in Canada that I believe the villagers here are getting used to it. Everyone has treated me well these past few months."

"But you have Richard."

"Yes, that's so. And I know folks are still suspicious of his brother, because Stephen voluntarily stayed with the Algonquin when he could have come home. But Charles escaped on his own, and I'm sure the people respect him for his initiative. He's clever and diligent. He would make you a good husband." Sarah placed a clump of wool between her cards and scraped the two paddles across each other, untangling the fibers.

"I suppose Charles and I do understand one another better than some," Jane conceded.

"Is it the thought of marriage in general that distresses you?" Sarah asked. "I don't mean to probe, but I have wondered. I've thought sometimes you weren't happy as Madame Robataille."

"I wasn't. But I had no choice. Jacques Robataille arranged it somehow with the French authorities before I even met him. I was staying for a time with a family in Quebec. For four months, I scrubbed their floors and washed their clothes. It was hard work, but no harder than what I'd done while indentured. Then one day, I was told to gather my things, for a voyageur had come for me and I was to be married that day."

"How horrible."

"Yes." Jane laid her sewing down in her lap. "He took me to his farm, and three days later he left me there alone for two months while he went on a trading voyage. I was terrified, but I didn't dare leave. He'd told me to tend the fields and livestock until he returned. If I didn't, he said he would beat me. I believed him. After all, he'd beaten me our first night together." She stared into the coals in the fireplace before them and clamped her lips together.

"Oh, Jane, I'm so sorry."

Jane's eyes burned. Hot tears spilled over her eyelids and streamed down her cheeks. She dashed at them with the back of her hand. "I shouldn't have said anything. I never have before . . . to anyone."

"Did he ever strike you again?"

"Every time he was home. It was a regular thing. When he wasn't happy, he boxed my ears. When he was drunk, it was worse."

Sarah sniffed. "And to think I considered my lot in the Pennacook village a harsh one. I can see now why the idea of marrying again is distasteful to you. But I'm positive Charles would never treat you so."

Jane inhaled deeply and wiped another tear away with her sleeve. "You are probably right."

"Give it time, dear," Sarah said softly.

Jane managed a shaky smile. "I believe I shall. Who knows what the Almighty may have in store for me? Now what are we going to cook for your husband's dinner?"

Two weeks later, Charles waited near the bottom of the meetinghouse steps for Jane to come out.

Ben Jewett had spread ashes on the icy steps that morning so the parishioners wouldn't slip on them, but the sun had been at work during the lengthy sermon and melted most of the ice from the treads.

Waiting for Jane to leave the building after services had become a habit, and she did not seem displeased when she came through the doorway and saw him standing there.

Goody Jewett came first, carrying the new baby. Jane and Christine followed her, herding the older children down the steps.

"Good day," he said to the pastor's wife, offering his hand to guide her down the stairs.

"A good day, indeed, Charles," Elizabeth replied with a broad smile.

"Miss Miller . . . Jane." He lowered his voice. "Might I call on you this evening?"

She stopped for a moment, holding Constance's hand tightly as the little girl tugged toward the street and home.

For an instant Charles feared she would say no. She could end his pursuit of her in a second. She had only to refuse his company, and he would not venture near the parsonage again.

She glanced about then spoke softly. " 'Tis lovely weather today. Perhaps . . . we could walk this afternoon?"

Gladness shot through him. This was progress. Evenings at the parsonage were not unpleasant, but with winter's cold came togetherness most of the time. The parson had left off studying at the chilly meetinghouse, and the last time Charles ventured to call on Jane, all eight of the Jewetts and Christine Hardin had shared the great room of the cottage for two hours. It was impossible ever to speak a private word to Jane.

It would be nice to have the object of his admiration alone for a few minutes. Even if they stayed within the sight of the critical villagers, they could at least distance themselves from other people enough so that they could converse in private. "I shall come by in two hours' time, if that is agreeable to you."

She nodded but did not smile.

As she let Constance lead her away, he stared after her, regret and anticipation struggling in his heart. He wished she would smile more. Sarah Dudley smiled all the time now. He would have to ask Richard what he had done to put that gleam of happiness on Sarah's face.

Other people had passed him by, and the Reverend Jewett came last down the steps.

"Good day, Charles. Will you take dinner with us?"

"Thank you, sir, but the Dudleys have invited me." Charles fell into step with the pastor. "Sir, may I have a confidential word with you?"

"Of course."

Charles cleared his throat. "I've given it a great deal of thought, and I'd like to offer Miss Miller my hand in marriage, if that meets your approval."

"I have no objection, though we would miss her sorely. She's become a part of our family."

"Aye, sir, I can see that, and it's why I come to you as I would her father. She said she would walk with me this afternoon, and I thought to ask her then."

The pastor eyed him thoughtfully. "Then I shall tell her before you come that she would do well to accept. However, she can refuse you if she wishes. My wife and I do not mind if she wants to remain in our household awhile longer."

"I understand, sir."

"Good. Of course there will be talk — nay, there is already talk — in the village about the two of you. There be those who question your character and hers both, because of your time spent in Canada. Don't listen to gossip, Charles. Miss Miller is a fine young woman."

"Aye, she is diligent. I've seen that."

"And she is true to her faith," the pastor added, "despite what some may think. Her brief marriage to the papist . . . well, that is regrettable. I don't know if she's told you, but she explained to my wife that it was all arranged without her consent. A rather trying time she had, I'm afraid."

"Yes, sir. I understand." Charles left him to walk out to Richard's house for dinner, thinking all the while of what the minister had said. He had considered Jane's status as a widow, and how that might affect her choice of a new husband. She seemed more independent and less eager to marry than most single women. He hoped his patient suit had overcome that tendency. However, he hadn't for a minute thought her religious past might keep them apart.

True, in Quebec she'd married a man of a different faith, but as the pastor had pointed out, that did not mean she had changed her own beliefs. And Pastor Jewett would never recommend that a man of his flock marry a woman whose faith was at question.

Nay, if she turns me down, it won't be for spiritual concerns. But she might find a hundred other reasons to reject me.

The sunlight sparkled on the snow as Jane and Charles strolled toward the river. Although it was the third of February, Jane's cloak kept her warm in the balmy air. She let her shawl fall off her hair and rest on her shoulders. It was so good to get out in the fresh air after being cooped up through weeks of cold weather.

"I expect we'll get more snow before

spring," Charles said.

"Aye," Jane agreed. "Winter's back is not broken yet. But it's nice to have a few warm days."

"I heard that a ship put in at Portsmouth with goods from England. The trader leaves at first light with his sled to go fetch some new stock."

"Ah. The trading post will be overrun when he returns."

Charles pointed ahead of them. "It's been so warm, the river's breaking up."

They had approached the riverbank, and Jane saw that already the ice had given way where the current was strongest, and a slash of dark water showed in the middle of the frozen stream. Likely another cold snap would freeze it again before long.

Charles kicked at the snow and stooped to pick up a stone. He threw it hard, and it flew out onto the ice.

"I'd like to marry you, Jane."

She caught her breath. The parson had forewarned her, but even so her mouth went dry and her heart pounded furiously. "This is rather sudden, Goodman Gardner."

"Forgive me. It does not seem that way to me."

"No?"

"I've thought of it for months."

She walked slowly along the riverbank, where other feet had trampled a path in the snow. Mixed feelings warred in her heart. She liked what she knew of him, but would he make a good husband? And did she want a husband at all? Not if he turned out like Jacques Robataille. She had long ago made that decision. She didn't want a mean man or one who would leave her to cope on her own for months at a time.

But Charles seemed unlike Monsieur Robataille. The first time she had met her Canadian husband — an hour before the wedding, she recalled bitterly — she had feared him, a feeling that never entirely left her until he was buried. She never wanted to be in a situation again where she could not control her own circumstances. Of that she was certain.

Charles was waiting for an answer, walking slowly along beside her and flicking an uncertain glance her way now and then.

"I . . ." She clamped her lips together.

"I admire you greatly, Jane, and I think we would suit."

"Do you?" She hated the way her voice cracked.

"Surely. We are much alike, you and I."

"How so?"

He stopped walking, and she did, too.

He stood looking down at her, a faint smile upon his lips. "We have both felt the stigma of being outcasts of sorts, because of the time we spent in Canada."

"That at least is true," she acknowledged.

He bowed slightly. "You know I was chosen last year to help negotiate for you and the other captives because I knew the language and culture of the savages. It was an advantage to the negotiators. But my skills, if you call them that, are not respected in Cochecho. The upright citizens still perceive me as half wild."

Jane knew he was right, even though many of the town's leading citizens seemed to accept Charles now. The elders had made a concerted effort to integrate him into the community when they granted him the status of freeman and allowed him to retain his father's land.

She looked up into his soft brown eyes. He waited patiently for her response, and she couldn't help feeling drawn to him. She had been skeptical at first, but after spending several hours with him during the past few weeks, she was beginning to know his mannerisms and opinions. She'd found no cause to dislike him. In fact, it seemed that the more time she spent with him, the better she liked him. But did she want to bind herself to him legally for the rest of her life?

She swallowed hard. "I will consider your proposal, Goodman Gardner."

His smile wavered, and he nodded. "Charles, please, or Charlie if you like. Thank you. That is all I ask. Please tell me when you have reached a decision."

As they ambled back toward the village, he unfolded to her his plans for his farm, and Jane listened eagerly. He was trapping furs to earn money for livestock and improvements to his property — property of which she might one day soon be mistress. The idea did not repel her. In fact, when he mentioned the possibility of purchasing foundation stock for a small flock of sheep, she entered into a deep discussion of wool culture.

"And do you spin and weave?" he asked.

"I do, sir. Not so well as Christine does, but I'm a fair hand at it."

"Richard and his father have pledged to help me expand my cabin as soon as the snow is gone. And I hope to add cattle soon. I'm a hard worker, Jane."

"Aye, so I'm told."

When they reached the parsonage, Goody Jewett invited him in for a cup of chocolate, a treat that Goodman Otis had brought them that morning, along with a joint of venison.

An hour passed quickly in lively conversation with the family. Even Christine offered a comment or two.

Jane realized how well Charles fit in with their little circle. She felt almost at ease with him here. But could she be comfortable with him alone in his remote cabin?

She pondered the topic for a fortnight. He came faithfully on Thursday and Sunday. After several more evenings spent with him by the Jewetts' hearth, Jane at last concluded that she knew her own heart.

FIVE

"Do you love him?" Sarah asked.

Jane frowned and took a few stitches in the apron she was hemming for Constance Jewett. "That will follow, don't you think?"

"Perhaps. Did it in your first marriage?"

Jane said nothing, for the only true answer would not be to her friend's liking.

Sarah's brow puckered. "I don't wish to see you wed a second time without love."

"How many women love the men they marry?"

"So speaks a woman who has never known true love."

Jane chuckled. "That is true. But I think love is rare. I see it between you and Richard, aye, and between Elizabeth Jewett and the reverend, when it comes down to it. They care deeply for one another. But I can't say that is the norm. Charles says we suit, and we are both diligent. We shall build up his farm together, and he shall strive to keep me in reasonable comfort. I've come to believe he is a decent man and will treat me kindly. That is all I hope for."

Sarah shook her head. "You aspire to so little. But I trust Charlie will teach you very soon how much more there is to marriage."

"I didn't come to hear you lecture me." Jane laid down her sewing and pretended to scowl at her friend.

"Indeed. You came to help me prepare dinner for my husband and his dearest friend and to deliver your answer to your suitor. Come. Let us start the corn bread baking. And I think we might make an apple pudding. Charlie is very fond of it. What say you?"

"I say I shall have to learn all his likes and dislikes." Jane stood and grasped her friend's arm. "Sarah, thank you for inviting me. I shouldn't like to have to accept his proposal under the eye of half a dozen or more chaperones."

Sarah hugged her. "You're most welcome. And I shall look forward with joy to the day you are my close neighbor. Come. Richard and Charlie have been hauling out logs for your new barn all morning, and they'll be here soon."

"*My* barn?"

"Of course. For the cow and sheep Charlie will buy you."

"Oh dear. I don't wish for him to think he must spend all his money to make me happy," Jane said. "It's not my intent to be a burden to him."

"It is a burden he will take on most gleefully."

Two hours later, when their dinner was finished, Charles offered to walk Jane back to the parsonage. She accepted, knowing this was the time they both craved for a private talk about their future.

Richard's detailed description of the projects he helped Charles undertake had sobered Jane. They were doing all this work for her — to make her comfortable should she accept Charles's suit. She couldn't turn him down now. He'd worked too hard to please her. Not that she wanted to reject him. But still, Sarah's prodding bothered her. What if she couldn't love Charles? What if they married and made a good effort, but she never knew that satisfaction Sarah spoke of — the knowledge that she loved her husband second only to God?

As they said their good-byes to Richard and Sarah, Jane couldn't keep back the dark thoughts. They were unworthy thoughts, she was sure. After all, Charles was a good man, and as such, he deserved more. She would give him unswerving loyalty and all the work her strength could give. But was it enough?

They walked along the path, past Richard's parents' stockaded house. The chilly air and low gray clouds told her that a storm was coming.

"I hope you get home safely, before the snow begins," she told him.

"Don't worry. I think it will hold off another hour, and that's plenty of time."

They walked on in silence for several yards.

"Goodman — Charles," she ventured.

"Yes, Jane?" He stopped in the path and drew her around to face him.

"I have considered your offer." She looked deep into his dark eyes, and she thought she saw anxiety that belied his outward calm.

"And?"

"If you . . . if you still feel the same way . . ."

"I do, Jane."

She nodded. "I'm not sure I can be the sort of wife you want. But I'll do my best. I'll work beside you, and —"

He pulled her into his arms, and she gasped as he engulfed her in his embrace. "Thank you. You've made me very happy, and you shan't regret it. Ever. I promise,

84

dear Jane."

He held her for a long moment, and she kept her face turned away from his. She couldn't bear to look into his intent eyes again. He felt more than she did, and it made her feel guilty. Did he want to kiss her now? She hoped not. The thought of his cold lips against hers unnerved her, reminding her of Jacques's unwanted kisses. She shivered.

"It's cold," Charles said. "I'll take you home."

"Thank you."

He drew her hand through his arm and held it in the crook of his elbow. Through his leather mittens and her wool ones, a bit of warmth transferred from his fingers to hers.

"If you'd like, I shall ask the Jewetts to bring you out to my farm next week and look it over. You can tell me if you'd like anything done different before — before we —" He flashed a glance down at her. "When do you wish to be married?"

"At your leisure," she murmured.

"The first of March perhaps? Or is that too soon?"

The date he selected was only a fortnight hence. It startled her to think she would have only two weeks left with the Jewetts to prepare her meager trousseau and settle her mind to being a wife again.

"If you wish it," she managed.

He squeezed her hand. "If you'd rather, I can wait longer, but I'd like to have you settled before planting time. And if you want me to complete the barn or add another room to the cabin first, Richard and I can —"

"No, Charles. March the first is fine."

He smiled radiantly down at her, and she was glad she had answered as she did. A man so transparently happy couldn't be cruel. She'd never seen him angry, but didn't all men show rage at times? Her father had. Mr. Plaisted, her former master, had. Jacques Robataille had. Even the Reverend Jewett's eyes went steely hard the day Sarah told him how a villager had insulted her and Jane, and Richard had knocked the man down for it. There was no doubt in her mind that Charles Gardner had a temper, though she hadn't seen it yet. Still, Charles seemed a pleasant young man who did not anger easily.

Jane realized vaguely that the line between righteous ire and cruelty wasn't entirely clear in her mind. Best to think of other things. "You needn't buy a cow right away," she told him.

"Oh, but we'll want milk and cheese."

"A goat?" She looked up at him, and something stirred inside her when he smiled and patted her hand.

"Nay. We shall have a cow. Captain Baldwin has a fine heifer I've got my eye on. When I sell my furs, there should be plenty for that and the supplies we'll need to get through until harvest."

"And you'll be putting in corn this spring?"

"Aye, and we'll plant you a kitchen garden. You tell me what you want, and I'll trade for the seed."

By the time they reached the village, Charles's enthusiasm spread to Jane. She entered into the planning of her vegetable garden. They spoke of herbs for which she could get seeds from Elizabeth and Sarah and the special variety of beans Goodman Heard had grown last year.

Charles's gentle voice lulled Jane, and she thought it was a voice she could listen to willingly for years to come. Knowing he was happy brought her a measure of happiness, as well, and she barely noticed the tall figure approaching the parsonage from the river path.

"Someone's calling for the parson," Charles noted, nodding toward the Jewetts' front yard.

Only then did Jane focus on the man approaching the little house. In an instant something familiar about the figure struck her, and her steps faltered.

"Jane?" Charles stopped walking and looked down at her anxiously. "What is it?"

"It can't be."

The man raised his fist and pounded on the door of the parsonage. Ben Jewett opened the door, and the man's voice came to them from fifty yards away, through the crisp, clear February air. "I've business with the minister."

Instantly Jane recognized the haughty voice. She felt light-headed and grasped Charles's sleeve.

"I thought he was dead."

"Who?" Charles's faced blanched, and he shot a glance toward the stranger. "Surely that's not . . . No. Not Robataille."

Jane pulled cold air into her lungs. "Nay. Nay, not he. Jacques Robataille is truly dead. I saw him buried. But, Charlie! It's Mr. Plaisted, my old master."

Charles stepped in front of Jane, instinctively placing himself between her and the stranger, blocking the man's view of her should he turn around.

The parsonage door was flung wide, but instead of admitting the caller as Charles had expected, the Reverend Jewett stepped outside onto the doorstone and closed the door. His voice was just low enough that Charles couldn't make out what he said, but when the stranger replied, there was no doubt.

"Where is she? Why was I not informed?"

The bits and pieces Jane had told him over the past few weeks came back to Charles's mind with a clarity that chilled him. *I was indentured . . . seven years . . . I had only a year left to serve.*

He turned, keeping his body in the line of vision between Jane and the men at the parsonage door. "You must keep out of sight until I see what he wants." Her gray eyes were full of fear. Charles grasped her hands and squeezed them. "Goody Deane's cottage is near. Slip in there and visit with the old woman while I go and speak to Parson Jewett and your —" He couldn't bring himself to say *your master,* so he amended his words. "And this man . . . I will see what he wants, and when he's gone, I shall come and get you."

Jane swallowed hard. He thought for a moment she would argue. Instead, she turned swiftly, lifting her skirt a couple of inches, and dashed the few yards to old Goody Deane's door, across the snow-covered street from the parsonage.

Charles watched while she knocked. When the door opened and Jane was safely inside the widow's home, he squared his shoulders and turned toward the pastor's cottage.

He assumed a leisurely pace as he approached the two men. The pastor glanced up when he turned in at the path to the parsonage and nodded but kept on speaking to the stranger.

"I assure you, sir, Miss Miller did not willfully deprive you of her labor. When she came to us, she believed you and your wife were murdered at Waldrons' garrison the same night she was captured. If we'd known otherwise, our town elders would have sent word to you to come and claim her."

The other man shook his head. "I've made no secret of the fact I am alive. Apparently Miss Miller has lived here the better part of a year, when she ought to have been keeping house for me. I call that grounds to extend her indenture. Where is she? I shall take her back with me today, and she can begin serving out the time she owes me."

"Please, sir, be reasonable," Samuel Jewett said. "Miss Miller was only a girl when the massacre occurred, and she was in a strange place. She was carried off to Quebec and kept there five years. When she returned, we offered her sanctuary here, along with others who had no family to claim them. Her parents had died previously, and she had no idea her employer still lived."

"Nor I that she survived. My wife was killed that night, sir. No trace was found of Jane. I supposed the Indians took her, but whether she lived or nay, I neither knew nor, to be frank, cared for some time. My injuries were grave, and I grieved my wife. While the servant girl's fate concerned me, other things claimed my attention — my health, my children, my business."

"Of course, sir."

Charles eased around closer to the pastor so that he could observe the man's face while he talked.

Plaisted took a crumpled pamphlet from his pocket. "And then I read this history of Cochecho captives, and there is the name of my servant. I repeat, Mr. Jewett, where is my property? I expect we are in for some foul weather, and I wish to make it to Dover Point tonight so I can take a ship to my home in Gloucester tomorrow."

Pastor Jewett threw Charles a noncommittal glance before he spoke. "She is not here at the moment, sir. She went earlier today to visit with friends outside the village. If the weather does indeed turn inclement, I would expect her to stay with them overnight."

"What? Where is this house she's at? Tell me at once, and I'll go there and fetch her!"

"Calm yourself, sir." Jewett looked up at the clouds and frowned. "This be not a good night to travel, I fear. You had best go to the ordinary and bespeak a bed there. I can send to the farmhouse and see if Miss Miller plans to return this eve."

A snowflake landed squarely on Plaisted's beaver hat.

"Just tell me where it is," Plaisted said. "If you're not forthcoming, I shall find a constable to intervene in this."

"Please, sir," the parson said. "Miss Miller will do what is right, I'm sure. There's no need for legal action. Let me establish whether she is coming home tonight. I will find you at the tavern and let you know when you may see her tomorrow."

Plaisted eyed him coldly for a moment. "I suppose it would be too late to journey back tonight. I can depend on you to bring me word this evening?"

"You may," said Jewett.

Plaisted nodded. He glanced briefly at Charles but said not a word to him. He turned and walked to the street and off toward the ordinary near the river.

Pastor Jewett gave a deep sigh. "You heard?"

"I did," Charles said.

"And where is Miss Miller? I dared not speak to you whilst the man lingered. Is she safe?"

"Did you not see her duck into Goody Deane's cottage these ten minutes past?"

"Nay. She knows her old master has come seeking her, then?"

"As we came from Richard Dudley's house, she recognized the man who knocked on your door. When she told me who he was, I bid her pay a call on the Widow Deane until I tell her to come forth."

"Well done." Jewett smiled at him. "So what's to be done now, Charles?"

"I intended to step into your house this afternoon and ask whether you might perform a marriage ceremony March the first. But this could change things."

The pastor frowned. "March first . . . nay, that is too soon. I must read the banns two Sundays."

"I would say March the fourth, then, if not for this fellow who wants to steal Jane away from me."

"You did well to keep silent. I wish you all

the best, but we must straighten this other matter out." Pastor Jewett glanced toward the house where Jane had taken refuge. "I'm thankful I did not see her, for I was able to truthfully tell the man she was a distance away. Let me speak to Jane and find how she was situated before her sojourn in Canada."

As they walked to Goody Deane's little house together, the pastor said regretfully, "When I penned that pamphlet last fall, I meant it only as a help to the young ladies, so they would become better understood by their neighbors. I never imagined it would bring harm."

"It's not your fault, sir. God knew your intentions." Charles knocked on the widow's door.

Jane opened it, peeking out timidly. "Where is he?" she asked.

"Gone to the ordinary for the night," said Charles.

The pastor stepped up beside him. "Come along home now, Jane, and we'll talk about this."

The widow's quavering voice came from within. "Parson, you can speak here without the distraction of the children. Miss Jane told me what's afoot. You ought to step in and thrash this out."

Jewett smiled at Charles. "Shall we?"

"If Jane doesn't mind, it would be more private, sir. Not that your family would matter, but . . ."

"But it might be easier for Jane if we keep this among us few," Jewett replied.

"Thank you, sir." Jane opened the door wider, and the two men entered. The snow fell thickly now, and they shook off the loose flakes as they passed through the doorway.

Goody Deane bade them sit, and she hobbled to a shelf. "Cider, that's what you need."

Charles glanced about the dim little room, which was nearly bare, and decided that offering cider to three callers would cut deeply into the widow's supplies. But they could not insult her by refusing. He tucked away a plan to bring her a bag of parched corn and some dried apples before the week was out.

"Now, Jane," the pastor said, "you told us recently that you were indentured as a girl. You saw the man who came to my house just now?"

"Aye, sir. That be my old master, Gideon Plaisted."

"You told us he and his wife were killed in the massacre."

Jane's lip trembled. "So I believed, sir.

When Captain Baldwin redeemed me in Quebec, he asked if I had any kin. I told him about my parents' deaths and how I was bound to Mr. Plaisted. He recalled that Mr. and Mrs. Plaisted both were slain in the massacre. Indeed, I saw the savages hack at the master as they dragged me away, sir." Tears filled her eyes. "I never imagined he lived and that I owed him my labor. Please, sir, I speak the truth. You have treated me kindly, and I would not deliberately mislead you."

Charles's heart went out to her. He reached over and took her hand. She sniffed and did not pull away, but her gray eyes swam with tears.

Goody Deane set two mugs and a small firkin on the table and, with shaking hands, poured out the cider. They all thanked her and took a sip.

"Mr. Jewett," Charles said, "could we not get the town elders and talk to this man? Surely he must see that it would not be reasonable to ask Jane to go back and work another year for him now."

The pastor shook his head. "I don't think so, Charles. The man does have a legal right to Miss Miller's labor. And if the magistrate believed she intentionally withheld her whereabouts from her master, he might extend her term of indenture."

Jane stared at him, and tears coursed down her cheeks. "Please don't let me go back, sir. He is a cruel man. I was beaten for the smallest things. The girl, Betty, who watched the children, was whipped for letting the little boy run off. The child was found safe, but Betty was hurt so badly she kept her bed for near a month. Then the master took her to court and got the magistrate to add the lost time to her papers."

The pastor stood and paced the room.

The widow had retreated to her hearth, where she sat hunched on a stool, muttering and stabbing at the coals with a poker. "Not right, not right," said Goody Deane.

Charles cradled Jane's hand in both of his. "I shan't let him take you away, dear," he whispered.

Jane caught her breath, and he felt a slight pressure from her fingers. Her touch gave him joy, though he feared he might lose her. Whatever happened, he determined not to let Plaisted take her away with him.

The thought of taking her back to Richard and Sarah's house and asking them to hide her crossed his mind, but immediately he discarded it. The pastor would never agree to deception, and Charles knew he couldn't put forth such a plan to Richard, either. Whatever they did must be done honestly.

"Charles, the storm is like to grow worse," said the pastor. "If you stay any longer, you won't get home tonight."

"I shall not leave the village with this unsettled, sir."

"You've no livestock to tend?"

"Not yet, sir."

Jewett nodded. "You are welcome to sleep at my hearth with my sons."

"Thank you."

"Then let us take Jane home to my wife and seek out another man to go with us and speak to this Gideon Plaisted. The captain, perhaps. His authority might stand us in good stead."

"What shall you say to him?" Jane asked. She clung to Charles's hand, and he was not displeased.

"We shall reason with him," the pastor replied.

"What if he will not change his mind?"

"Fret not. Ask God to guide us, and if this Plaisted refuses to listen to us, the Almighty will put the needful words in my mouth."

Jane raised her chin. "I do not mind working when I should, sir."

"I know you don't," said Jewett.

"But if his wife be dead . . ." She shook

her head. "He is a cruel one."

Charles stoked the widow's fire before they left, and the three walked in silence across to the parsonage. The pastor quickly told his wife their errand, and he and Charles left once more, going out again into the fast-falling snow. Dusk had fallen early, and there was no moon, but neither was there much wind. Charles felt that the storm would pass before morning.

They went first to Baldwin's house and asked the captain to accompany them. As they walked, Jewett again told the tale of Jane Miller's indenture and the arrival of her erstwhile master in the village.

"I can scarcely credit it," Baldwin said. "I was sure that man died. Ah, me. Perhaps I be partly at fault. I told the lass when we redeemed her that he had died. I'd no idea it wasn't so."

"He seems to have been gravely injured and took some time to recover," the pastor said. "And he told me when he first introduced himself that he no longer lives at Dover Point. He removed to Gloucester after he recovered from his wounds. Surely if he had not moved, he would have heard of Miss Miller's return last spring."

"Aye." The captain shook his head. "And she wishes not to go with him?"

"Nay, she implies he mistreated her when she was in his employ."

"She wishes to stay on with your family, then?"

Jewett smiled and nodded toward Charles. "In truth, she wishes to stay here and marry this stout young man, but we've not given Plaisted knowledge of that fact."

Baldwin grinned. "So! Going to settle down, are you, Charlie? We'll have to see that the bride stays in New Hampshire colony, then." He clapped Charles on the shoulder. "Don't worry, lad. I shan't let him talk round me. Your sweetheart has endured enough."

At last they came into the ordinary. Plaisted sat near the fireside in the public room, and Jewett made straight for him.

Plaisted stood. "Well, Reverend, what say you? Will Miss Miller be ready to travel with me in the morn?"

"Nay, sir, I think not." Jewett gestured toward Baldwin. "This man be one of our constables and captain of our militia. It is his opinion, having been instrumental in retrieving Miss Miller from the French, that she should be free now and her obligation forgiven."

"Nonsense." Plaisted's face darkened, and he glared at Captain Baldwin. "I have a legal right here."

"You do, sir," the captain said smoothly, "but the moral thing would be to release this young woman who has borne already much sorrow and hardship."

"Sorrow? Hardship? What of myself? I was injured. My wife was slain before my eyes."

"It is not up to Miss Miller to compensate you for your losses," Baldwin countered.

"You don't understand, sir," cried Plaisted. "This woman owes me a year's labor. A magistrate will find in my favor. She is my property for a minimum of twelve months. I have the document here."

Charles's heart sank as the man drew a folded parchment from his waistcoat.

"And the judge might well find that she should give me another nine months' work for the time she's spent here idle without my knowing it. Or even for the five years she spent in Canada."

Charles opened his mouth and closed it again. The man was mad! Could he hope to claim Jane's labor for years to come? He looked to the pastor for help.

"Sir," Jewett began, "it is possible for a master to sell a servant's indenture to another. Would you put a price on the year's contract Miss Miller left outstanding with you when she was captured?"

"A price?" Plaisted eyed him coolly.

"That is not a bad idea," Baldwin said. "State the value of her work, sir."

"I had not thought to sell the contract."

"But you could hire another maid with the money," Jewett said.

Plaisted scratched his chin. "Nay, I think not. Now that my wife is gone, it would be too hard to break in new domestic help. I had another hired girl, and she took sick last winter and died. Nay, Miss Miller is strong, and she's survived the hardships, as you put it, of captivity. She must be a tough one."

"But she has a new life here now," Pastor Jewett said. "Surely we can reach an agreement. There must be some way you can release her from this debt."

Plaisted looked the parson in the eye. "There be only one way, sir. If Jane Miller will marry me, then I shall forgive her debt."

Six

Jane went about her morning chores with a heavy heart. The pastor's report the evening before had chilled her to the bone. Marry Gideon Plaisted or go back and work for him for at least a year. She had lain awake most of the night, pondering the alternatives and begging God for a solution.

The fact that Charles Gardner was missing from his spot on the hearth when she rose at dawn hadn't helped ease her mind. No doubt he'd gone to check his trapline, but she had counted on having a word with him before the men went to settle things with Plaisted.

"I expect he'll be back ere long," the minister had told her. "But Baldwin has promised to go with me, and he thought to ask Mr. Heard to go with us, too. They'll come here, and we shall all go together to the ordinary. We shall do all we can to aid your cause."

Jane was not comforted. She had seen Plaisted beat Betty years ago, and he had even struck Jane at times, as well. It was all she had needed to teach her to be nimble and keep out of his way as much as possible. Marry the man? Never!

As she stoked the fire and cooked corn mush for breakfast, she prayed. Christine knew of her dilemma, and every time Jane looked her way, she saw that Christine's lips moved in silent prayer as she worked, tending the baby and dressing the Jewett girls. Together they put the last touches on the morning meal while Abby set the table for the first round of breakfast.

Pastor Jewett came in from outside with two pails of water from the river, poured the contents of one into the big kettle, and moved the crane into position over the fire to heat the water for dishes and laundry. In spite of her crisis, the routine of the family went on. Ben and John filled the wood box, and at last Christine sat down with Mr. Jewett and his wife, Ben, John, and Ruth. Jane and Abby served them their meal, while Constance helped by wiping up the spills around Ruth's stool.

As soon as the boys and Christine finished eating, Jane quickly rinsed their dishes for the second sitting. She sat down with the girls to eat, but she had no appetite. Christine brought her a bowl of mush, a hot biscuit, and a cup of weak tea brewed from blackberry leaves. Jane sighed and forced down a bite.

Pastor Jewett lingered at the table, though Elizabeth went to the corner to nurse the baby.

"There must be a solution to this, Jane. I know you don't wish to marry this man." The pastor held up his cup so Christine could refill it with tea.

"I would die first." Jane stared down at her food. She could feel the parson's disapproving frown, but he did not scold her for speaking so.

"If you must go with him, I shall insist upon the terms being written out clearly. He can't keep you for more than a year."

"Can't he?" Jane felt tears spring to her eyes. "He is a cruel man, sir. If he wants to bind me longer, he will find a way." The law stated that indentures who ran away could have their terms of bondage doubled.

Beyond that, she dared not think or speak of the way Betty had been abused. When she was found to be with child, Betty was denied her freedom, even though her term of indenture had ended. The law said indentured servants who became pregnant must continue in servitude. Jane was a young girl when Betty's plight was discovered, and she'd heard Betty weep night after night in the attic they shared. Jane had never known who fathered Betty's child, but she had her suspicions. And Mr. Plaisted was widowed now. Perhaps marrying him would be better than being merely his servant once more. Jane shuddered at the thought.

A loud knock on the door announced the arrival of Captain Baldwin and John Heard.

"Morning, Reverend," the captain called. "Are you ready to go and straighten this out?"

"I suppose so." Pastor Jewett pulled on his coat. "I hoped Charles Gardner would be here when we went, but he left early this morning and hasn't yet returned."

"Got a personal interest in this case, has he?" John Heard asked.

"Well, yes, in a manner of speaking. I suppose it's no secret, and I was going to read the banns at meeting Sunday."

Jane turned away and busied herself by adding wood to the fire so the men would not see her flushed face.

"I pray you still can," said Baldwin. "Those two young folks deserve a chance at a quiet life."

"Aye. It would be a pity if this interloper

spoiled things for them," Heard agreed.

"Miss Miller," the pastor called to her, "you keep close here with my wife. I shall return as soon as I am able to tell you the outcome."

She nodded and dropped a slight curtsy.

The door closed behind the men, and Christine came over and put her arm around Jane. "There now. God knows what is best."

"Aye, He does," Jane agreed.

"Come here, girls," Elizabeth called from her chair across the room. "Leave your work for a moment, and we shall pray together."

Jane and Christine gathered the children, and they all clustered about Elizabeth. The children sat on their parents' bed, and the two young women stood on either side of the mother. They had barely bowed their heads when the door burst open.

"Miss Miller! Jane!" The pastor surged through the door, followed by several others.

"What is it, Samuel?" Elizabeth asked, wrapping the baby's blanket closer about him. The small room seemed full of large men and overcoats.

"Wait until you hear. You won't believe it. No, wait. Charles shall tell it."

Captain Baldwin and John Heard stepped

aside, and Jane saw that Charles Gardner had entered with them. She took a hesitant step toward him.

"Come, come," the pastor said, pushing Charles forward. " 'Tis a most marvelous answer to prayer."

The others stood in silence. Charles looked down into her eyes, and Jane felt her hope rising.

"Is Mr. Plaisted willing to release me?" Her voice squeaked, and she looked down, almost fearing to hear the answer despite the parson's excitement.

"Aye," Charles said quietly. "Jane, you owe him nothing."

Her heart skipped a beat, and she felt light-headed. She raised her eyes to meet his soft gaze.

"How can this be?" Elizabeth asked, looking toward her husband. "Last night he ranted that he would take her with him today."

"So he did. And yet he's already left for Dover Point and shall journey on to Gloucester alone. Speak, Charles!" the pastor boomed.

Charles cleared his throat. "It was very simple, really. After thinking about it overnight, he was willing to be compensated for your time, Jane. I bought your indenture."

■ ■ ■ ■

Jane opened her eyes. She was lying on Goody Jewett's pallet in the corner, and half a dozen people stood staring down at her.

"There, child. You're all right. Just rest." Elizabeth looked up at the others. "Mr. Jewett, could you take the children out to play in the new snow? Jane needs a moment to recover herself."

"I shall go with them," Christine said.

She and the pastor quickly bundled the little ones, all but the baby, into their wraps and hustled them outside. The men melted away, too, except for Charles. He and Goody Jewett knelt beside her.

"My dear, do you feel well?" Elizabeth asked.

"Yes. I . . ." Jane closed her eyes again. She must have fainted, something she never did, not even when she had seen savages tomahawking her mistress and they had seized Jane and dragged her from the burning garrison.

"Speak to her, Charles," Elizabeth whispered.

"Jane." His voice cracked.

She looked up into his worried brown eyes. "Is it true?" she managed. "Am I bound to you now?"

He frowned and shook his head. "Nay. You are bound to no one. You are free, sweet Jane."

She exhaled and thought about that. "But how did you pay him? You hadn't sold your furs yet."

"I routed the trader out of bed, and he agreed to buy them early this morning. Then I went to the ordinary and woke Mr. Plaisted — rather rudely, I'm afraid."

Elizabeth gave a short laugh, and Jane smiled. "And that was enough?"

Charles shrugged and looked off toward the fireplace. "Nay, his price was more than I had."

"Then how —"

"Richard and his father. I ran to them, and they loaned me enough money. They said we can take as long as we need to pay them back, but it won't be long, Jane. Another good week on my trapline or, failing that, a good corn crop this summer."

"But, Charles, I'll never be able to pay you back, even if you can pay the Dudleys."

"Hush, none of that." He took her hand. "You're going to be my wife, remember? At least you said yesterday you would."

She nodded. "If you still want me."

"Of course I do."

Elizabeth eased away from them and took the baby over to the bench near the hearth.

Jane struggled to sit up, and Charles stuffed the feather pillows behind her.

"Charles, you don't have to marry me, you know. By all rights, I should work for you now. If you want it that way, I can spin and weave and cook for you for a year. You needn't marry a servant if you don't wish to."

"Stop. That's foolish talk."

"Not so foolish. Many folk would never think of marrying an indentured girl."

"Nay. Don't think that way, Jane. Half the men and women in this village were indentured in their youth. I didn't buy you to own you or to make a slave of you."

"Then why did you put yourself in debt for me?"

"Need I tell you? I love you, Jane."

She shut her eyes once more, but it was too late. Her tears flowed freely. "Charlie, I . . . I don't know what to say."

"Say you'll let the parson read the banns on Sunday. That nothing has changed between us."

"You hold my indenture. That paper . . ."

"That paper is nothing. I hold it only so that I can prove you are no longer bound to Plaisted. If I thought him an honest man, I would burn it before your eyes. But I fear we must keep it until the term of your indenture expires. Be that as it may, I'll do something else, Jane."

"What?"

"Legally, I'm your master now. I'll write another paper saying you are free, and you can keep it yourself, to look at whenever you want. If ever I ask you to work harder than you're capable of, or if ever I'm mean or short with you, you can take that paper out and remind me that you are a free woman."

She sat still for a moment. It was a wonderful thought, and yet something about it struck her as wrong.

"But I'll be your wife." She felt her face redden as she said it. "A wife should never claim freedom from her husband."

He captured her other hand and held them both in his. "Jane, dearest, I shall try to be the kind of husband from whom you never want your freedom."

His eyes glittered, and Jane felt a giddy anticipation. She didn't deserve such devotion. And Charlie! He deserved far more than she could give him. She would work, yes, whether she was free or not. She would give her strength to help him.

If only she could learn to love him.

■ ■ ■ ■

On a bitterly cold March morning, Jane and Charles stood before the Reverend Samuel Jewett in his home. Jane wore a new white linen shift stitched lovingly by Christine. She fingered the rich brown overskirt that was a gift from her friend Sarah Dudley. She had never had such a fine garment as that skirt. Richard, Sarah, Christine, and the Jewett family crowded around while the pastor conducted the wedding ceremony.

"Do you, Charles Gardner, take this woman to be your lawfully wedded wife?"

"I do." Charles stood stiff as a poker beside her.

"And do you, Jane Miller, take this man to be your lawfully wedded husband?"

Jane looked up at Charles. His large brown eyes regarded her solemnly.

"I do."

Her words were barely audible, but Charles's eyes leaped with joy. He smiled for the first time all morning and squeezed her hand. Jane felt light-headed, but she managed to smile back.

After the service, Richard and Sarah packed the bride and groom, with Jane's small bundle, into a sled pulled by Richard's father's oxen.

Richard's parents and sister, Catherine, met them at the gate of the Dudley family's stockade.

"You make a lovely bride," Catherine cried.

Jane kissed her and thanked her, but she felt out of place. Her unease increased as they sat down to eat the wedding breakfast with the Dudleys, including Richard's sixteen-year-old brother, Stephen.

The Dudleys' home, while not lavish, was three times the size of the parsonage and much more comfortable. These were her new neighbors, and Jane knew they would accept her with kindness, but her appetite fled. Had she made a mistake?

Charles knew about her background as an indentured servant and of her difficult marriage in Quebec. He had also gone through deep waters, but he seemed to have overcome past trials and was content now to go on with a quiet life as a settler on the New Hampshire frontier. Could she fit into that life with him and be the wife he needed?

Sarah must have read her discomfiture in her face, for after the meal, as the women put away the food and washed the dishes, she managed a quiet word with Jane.

"What is troubling you on this happy

day?" she asked.

"Oh, Sarah, I fear I've wronged Charles. I should not have married him."

"Why ever not? He loves you."

"Aye." Jane ducked her head. "It isn't fair to him that he can feel that way, and . . ."

"And you can't?"

Jane said nothing.

"Charles is a gentle man," Sarah said softly. "I'm sure in time your feelings will catch up with your knowledge of him."

"But he's given all the money he saved and more — gone into debt to Richard and his father for me. I come to Charles with only the clothes on my back, an extra shift, skirt, and bodice, and a small sewing kit that Elizabeth Jewett gave me."

"And a quilt." Sarah turned to a chest behind her and lifted a folded patchwork quilt. "This is a gift from the Dudley women."

Jane stared at the colorful material and reached out to stroke the woolen patches.

"Such fine stitching!"

Sarah smiled. "My mother-in-law and Catherine and I sewed it for you. Charles's cabin may be small, and it was stripped by natives during the massacre, but he has stocked it since his return. I'm sure you'll find adequate dishes and linens for the two of you. But if you need anything, do come and tell me. We shall share what we have until the two of you settle in and Charles's crops begin to profit you."

Jane nodded, still unsure she could be comfortable as a wife again, but this was not the place to express her doubts. Nor the time, two hours after her wedding.

Charles put the quilt with Jane's bundle into his pack, and the couple set out on foot with Richard and Sarah. The young Dudleys soon left them at their own house, and Jane trudged on behind her husband, feeling small and timid as they entered the forest.

The path between the two cabins was only a quarter mile but led through woods the men had not yet cut for firewood. Charles had mentioned to her that one day all his land would be cleared for fields, except perhaps for a narrow line of trees he would leave as a border to break the winter winds.

Jane had not left the village in ten months except for two visits to Sarah. Each time she got beyond hailing distance of the parsonage, goose bumps rose on her arms, and today was no exception. As they reached the tree line, Charles turned and smiled at her, waiting for her to catch up the few steps between them.

"Do I walk too fast for you?"

"Nay." Jane looked up at the bare limbs overhead. "Be these your trees or Richard's?"

"Ours." He shifted his musket to his other shoulder and held out his hand. "Walk beside me. The path is wide enough, and I want to watch your face when you see our farm for the first time."

Determined not to disappoint him, she plodded on, not pulling away from his touch. They broke out of the dim forest in a short time, and the wind caught at her cloak. Ahead lay a small, snug cottage of riven slab siding and a squat log barn with unroofed rafters rising against the gray sky.

"Richard and I will finish the barn before planting time," Charles said with evident pride. He looked at her anxiously. "What do you think?"

"It looks very fine."

He smiled and led her toward the cabin. "I banked the fire this morning, and it will be chilly inside, but I'll build it up for you straightaway."

Jane held her breath as he reached to open the oak plank door. She refused to make a mental comparison with the open fields and large outbuildings of the Robataille farm in Quebec. That was a place of fear and sorrow. This farm, however small and rough, would be a happier place if she made it so. Or so it would be, provided Charles did not reveal a darker side of which she was ignorant.

He threw the door open and stepped back, looking at her. She wondered for a second if he would pick her up and carry her over the threshold.

"Won't you come in, Goody Gardner?" His crooked smile almost calmed her, but then he pulled off his mittens and touched her cheek. "Welcome, dear wife."

Jane turned away to avoid his intent gaze and stepped up into the house. The one room was dim, lit only by the sunlight streaming through the door and that admitted by two narrow slits of windows in the side walls. The back wall was taken up entirely by a great fireplace.

She took a swift glance around. The room was neat, almost bare. She was pleased to see a rope bed frame next to one wall and a rectangular table and two benches in the center of the room. A rough settle stood by the hearth, and two kettles and a large skillet hung on pegs set in the stonework. At the other end of the room were a plain pine chest and a series of shelves that held dishes, boxes, small sacks, and crocks.

"Richard will help me add a room as soon as we can," Charles said.

Jane jumped at his nearness when he spoke and instinctively took a step away.

Charles rested his musket in a corner and took off his pack. He laid the quilt and her bundle on the bed. "I'll tend the fire."

She noted that a pile of wood filled a niche at one side of the fireplace, and a wooden bucket full of water sat near it.

She took a deep breath. "Shall I start dinner?"

"If you wish. You may hang your cloak and shawl here near the door." Charles went to the shelves and stored his pack away. "There be crockery here and linens in the chest."

She nodded.

He looked at her as though he would speak again then turned to the hearth.

Jane stood uncertainly, watching him stir up the coals and lay dry wood on them. The sticks began to crackle, and the flames flared.

Charles stood and faced her. He blinked, seeming surprised that she stood in the same spot where he'd left her. "I . . . have somewhat to tend to outside."

She wondered how many people she should prepare the midday meal for. "Be Richard coming today to work with you?"

119

"Nay. He will come tomorrow."

"Ah."

They looked at each other. Again Jane felt the uncertainty. She didn't belong here.

Charles turned and went out, closing the door behind him.

What on earth had she done? Tying herself to another man for the rest of her life had to be a mistake. She ought to have waited and insisted on more time to get to know Charles. And what if she conceived right away? Was she ready to undergo the rigors of childbirth again? On the other hand, what if she didn't? In the three years with Jacques Robataille, their only baby was stillborn. Was she capable of bearing a healthy child? Jane wondered if she had been remiss in not revealing this somber bit of information to Charles and letting him decide if he wanted a potentially barren wife.

She stood in the middle of her new house and slowly turned in a circle. It was no bigger than the parsonage, though the Jewetts had a bigger loft. She had expected this. It was dark, but that was probably because of the danger of living outside the village. Windows were only extra entrances for attacking savages. The slit windows in these walls would not allow any attackers to enter the house. Only the door would let them pass. That was reassuring. And the cabin seemed solid.

She took off her shawl and stepped to the pegs near the door. She hung the garment up and then put her cloak over it, leaving a peg free for her husband's coat when he came in from whatever it was he was doing outside. The room was still chilly, but the fire was gaining ground, and if she got to work, she would soon be warm.

A sudden curiosity prompted her to lift the latch on the only door and pull it toward her two inches. She peeked out through the crack but couldn't see a sign of Charles. She was about to close the door when she heard a quiet sound and looked toward the unfinished barn.

Charles came through the doorway carrying a huge reddish bundle. She gasped then exhaled slowly. A red fox carcass. His trapline, of course. He must be setting about to skin his latest catch. It would take many furs to make up for what he had spent to redeem her. Their plans to buy a heifer would have to wait.

Would he leave her here alone in the early mornings when he went to check his traps? And would he leave her a weapon to defend herself if savages came? Not that she knew how to use a gun.

She closed the door noiselessly and went to the bed. Untying her bundle, she shook out her extra clothes and laid the shift in the chest. Charles appeared to have an extra shirt and one extra pair of stockings there. She would see that he soon had more. Sarah had promised her some yarn.

She changed quickly out of the new wedding skirt. That would be her Sunday best. As she reached for the older, frayed, everyday skirt, her hand brushed the pocket tied about her waist. She reached into it and heard the stiff parchment crackle.

In the pocket were the three documents that determined the course of her life. Her indenture, which Charles had bought from Plaisted; the emancipation document he had presented to her that same day; and a copy of their marriage record, handed to her by the Reverend Samuel Jewett that morning.

She pulled on her gray wool skirt and smoothed its folds over her shift and pocket. As she tied her apron about her waist, she sent a prayer heavenward.

Almighty Father, I'm not sure I can be the kind of wife this man deserves. Please help me. Teach me all I need to know to be the best woman for Charles.

SEVEN

Charles wrapped the chain around the butt end of the big maple log and signaled to Richard to start the oxen. The big beasts strained against the yoke and slowly began to walk toward his house. The snow was melting fast, and soon it would be impossible to drag logs or sleds easily. They would have to wait out the mud season until summer to haul anything heavy in a cart.

When they reached the back of Charles's cabin, he swiftly unhooked the chain, releasing the log beside several others they had already brought out.

"Shall we stop for dinner?" Richard asked.

Charles looked anxiously up at his chimney. Smoke poured from it steadily, but Jane hadn't come out to tell them the meal was ready. Usually if she heard them enter the yard, she came out to announce dinner.

"Perhaps one more twitch?" Charles asked.

Richard pulled off his cap and wiped his brow. "Charlie, we've been working dawn to dusk for weeks. Is it vital we get all the logs out now? It won't hurt you to wait and build the extra room later in the year."

"I want to give this to Jane. You understand."

Richard nodded, and Charles felt he did understand. But still Richard seemed ready to take a rest from their labor. "I'm tired, Charlie. That's the long and the short of it."

Charles pulled off his mittens and sat down on the log. "I'm sorry. I've asked you for more than a fair share of work."

"Nay, you helped me as much last fall, when I was trying to get a nice home ready for Sarah before our wedding."

"But we also gave two full days' work last week to help the other men haul out logs for adding rooms to the parsonage. You helped me put up a barn for livestock I don't have yet, and we've cut enough firewood for the coming year for us and you and your father's household. I've overstepped our friendship."

Richard sighed. "I don't begrudge the work. We all work hard. Such is our lot in life."

"What is it, then? Not enough time with Sarah?"

"Perhaps." Richard eyed him keenly. "You're quiet lately, and I wonder about you."

"How so?"

"For a man married a mere fortnight, you're awfully solemn. Are things all right between you and Jane?"

He'd struck home, and Charles couldn't meet his piercing gaze.

Richard came over and stood squarely in front of him. "Charlie? What's wrong?"

Charles shrugged. "I wish I knew. Perhaps I shouldn't have pressed her to marry me so soon. But I left it up to her. And now she barely speaks to me."

"Do you talk at the supper table?"

Charles scowled at him. "What about?"

"Anything."

"I tell her how much wood we've cut. But . . . we don't say much, either of us. I don't know how to talk to her."

"You both speak English."

"That's very clever."

Richard smiled. "Yet you have no trouble talking to me."

"You stuck your nose in and wouldn't leave it alone."

"Ah. Well, women like to talk, Charlie."

"Not Jane."

"Oh, I'll warrant she does. Do you talk

125

about the farm?"

"A bit."

"Planned your garden?"

Charles shook his head. "Not yet."

"What about her housework?"

Charles gestured impatiently. "I let her run the house as she sees fit. I've tried not to make demands on her, so she could take her time settling in. She doesn't want to talk about sweeping and scrubbing."

"Maybe she does. My Sarah does."

That didn't seem right. Charles looked up at him. "Fascinating conversation at your house."

"No, really. I come in and wash up, and I tell her what I did that day. I tell her that the house smells lovely and ask her what she's been baking. And while we're at table, I ask her how her spinning went, and if she wasn't spinning that day, she tells me she was stitching or doing a wash or visiting my mother. It's all very nice between us. Leads to sweet talk."

Charles mulled that over. "Sounds delightful, but my Jane —" He broke off suddenly and jumped up as his wife stepped around the corner of the cabin.

"Dinner is ready." She didn't look at either of them.

"Thank you, Jane," Richard said with a

smile. "We'll un-hitch the oxen and wash up."

Jane disappeared silently around the corner.

Charles whirled to search Richard's face. "You don't think she heard, do you?"

Richard laughed. "No, I don't." His friend studied his face. "I'm sorry. I shouldn't have laughed. This isn't funny."

"No, it's not."

"Do you tell her you love her?"

Charlie winced. "I did once. When I bought her indenture. But she didn't answer me, and if she doesn't love me, I figure she doesn't want me to keep saying it. Oh, Richard!" He kicked at the log and jumped back in pain, hopping on one foot and holding the toe of his boot.

"Maybe she'd like to visit with Sarah more often."

"I've told her she can visit Sarah or her friends in the village anytime she wants, but she must tell me first so that I can escort her. I don't want her walking the paths alone."

"That's as it should be."

"I tell you, I will let her do whatever she wants, so long as she's happy as my wife. But she doesn't seem happy."

Richard nodded. "Come. She's waiting

dinner on us. Bring her to visit Sarah tomorrow." He reached to unfasten the bow pin that would release the near ox from its yoke.

"All right, and we'll take the day off from hauling logs. You need to catch up on chores around your place."

The two men left the oxen inside Charles's barn to munch the feed Richard had brought for them. When they went in the house, Charles saw that Jane had laid out the soap and a towel and poured clean water into the washbowl. He allowed Richard to wash his hands first then took his turn.

As he returned from tossing the water out the front door, he was startled to hear Jane talking to his friend. "Yes, I should like to very much. I'd feel easier when Charles is off checking his traps or working in the woods with you."

"You'd like to what?" Charles looked from Jane to Richard and back again.

"Jane would like to learn to shoot."

"To shoot?" Charles sat down hard in his chair at the head of the table. Jane had never uttered a word to him about shooting. Was she even strong enough to heft a musket? And when he was off in the woods, he took his gun with him anyway.

"Do you still have that old gun of your father's?" Richard asked, as though reading his thoughts.

"Nay. I expect the Pennacook took it in the raid, or else someone came after and took it. This house was stripped when I came back from my two years in Canada."

Richard nodded. "I'm thinking of getting an extra musket to leave with Sarah when I'm gone. The stockade I'm building will give her a measure of security, but I'm sure she'd feel better if she had a gun."

Charles eyed Jane skeptically. "You . . . really want to learn to shoot?"

"I would like to, sir. We be far from help if trouble should find us here." She looked up at him. Her gray eyes held a somber, determined look.

He wondered if there wasn't more to her story than he knew. "Well, I suppose I could teach you." His mind totted up what he could get for the furs. There was no way he could afford another musket. And he couldn't leave his gun at home when he went traipsing about the forest. That would be suicide. There must be some other way he could help her feel safe when she was alone at their house.

"What if I bring Sarah the first warm day and we'll have a shooting class?" Richard suggested.

"I suppose it couldn't hurt," Charles said.

"If nothing else, they'll be better able to help us reload if need be."

Jane smiled. "I should feel much more competent if I learned that skill."

"All right, then." Charles threw Richard a baffled glance. "If you have no qualms about it, then we'll do it."

The weather turned bitter in the night, and Jane was afraid Charles would refuse to take her to the Dudleys' the next morning. She rose early to fix breakfast and do her morning chores in the kitchen. When he asked if she wished to go in the cold, she stepped up eagerly. "I've looked forward to seeing Sarah. Do you mind awfully?"

"Nay. We'll go, then." He bid her bundle up warmly, and they swiftly walked the short distance.

Richard and Sarah welcomed them.

"It be too cold to work outdoors today," Richard said as Sarah took their wraps.

"Aye. The old year must go out with one last stretch of foul weather," Jane agreed.

"Let's hope April comes in with warmth," Sarah said. She went to the hearth and took a kettle of warmed cider off the fire. "Sit, Charles. You can help Richard fix my loom."

"Oh, I shan't stay that long. I've a score of beavers hung up in my barn to skin, and

I need to rive more shingles. I'll come back ere sunset for Jane."

"Take supper with us, then."

"Well, perhaps." He shot an anxious glance at Jane.

"If you think it's safe to walk through the woods after dark," she said.

He nodded. "All right, then."

Sarah handed him a steaming cup of cider and prevailed upon him to sit for a few minutes with them before heading home.

Jane enjoyed the morning, sewing with Sarah while Richard worked on the loom in the corner. The pleasant conversation with her hosts soon lifted the gloom that had hung over her.

When Richard went out to check on his livestock, Sarah fixed her with a meaningful look. "All right, tell me. How does the married life suit you?"

"I think . . ." Jane took a few stitches then looked up at her. "I believe I'm lonely."

"Lonely? But you've got Charlie!"

"I know. It seems silly, doesn't it? But we hardly exchange a dozen words each day, and he's out working all the time. Being here with you today, I feel entirely different than when I'm over there alone." She clamped her lips shut and bent over her work.

"I know Charles and Richard have been working hard lately," Sarah said. "Perhaps they need to stop getting wood out for a few days and give you and Charles time to be together."

"Oh, we are together," Jane said, thinking of the long, silent nights in the cabin.

"Richard says you want to learn to shoot."

"Aye."

"Because of the Indians?"

"I won't be taken again, Sarah."

A shadow crossed Sarah's face, and she nodded. "Agreed. Richard's father has an extra musket. He told Richard he could use it to teach me. Can Charles come up with a weapon for you?"

"I don't know. I don't like to ask him to spend more, but I do get fearful when he's gone for hours."

"I know," Sarah said. "I try not to think about it, but we're more isolated out here than my parents' home was in the village. If Indians came here, no one would hear us scream. Do you keep the door barred while Charles is out working?"

"Aye. When I hear him return, I unbar it. And I pray a lot. I also keep a butcher knife near as I work about the house."

Sarah sighed. "It's part of life in this place. I'm glad our husbands have been working

132

together of late. I know God doesn't wish us to live in fear, but experience teaches caution."

Jane set her jaw. She and Sarah both knew the horror of seeing loved ones killed and being forced to march off into the wilderness. "As I said, I will not be taken captive again."

"Let us talk of more pleasant things." Sarah settled back in her chair and picked up her knitting. "Knowing you are close by has made my days sweeter. Knowing Charles as we do, I expect he is kind to you."

"Aye. He's a very gentle man. He makes no demands on me, and he allows me to do just as I please."

"And this displeases you? You should be the happiest of women, I'd think."

Jane shrugged. "I don't know. I'm not used to it." She poked her needle through the material she held and sat back. "I've never been free before, except the months I lived with the Jewetts."

Sarah nodded. "We could have left anytime, but we didn't want to."

"I came to love them," Jane agreed. "Still, doesn't it grate on you as a married woman to be known about the village, not as Sarah Dudley or even Mrs. Dudley, but as Richard Dudley, his wife?"

Sarah frowned. "I've heard such things said. But it's just the way people speak. Women are part of their husbands' families. We bear their names and their identities."

"Doesn't that bother you? We can't own property."

"Do you want a farm of your own?"

"Nay, that's not what I meant."

"Then I misunderstand you. Jane, what is the trouble?"

Jane sighed and picked up her sewing. "I don't know."

"Is it that farm you lost in Quebec? It was bigger and grander than Charlie's, wasn't it?"

"That makes no matter. The price of being its mistress was higher than a woman should pay."

Sarah sat in silence for a moment. "I don't know all you suffered, to be sure. But I'm sorry. Sometimes I think my stay in the Pennacook village was an easy lot."

Jane shifted her position. Her own discontent rankled her. Sarah was right — she should be happy. She smiled across at her friend. "I am not ungrateful, and I don't say this to get your sympathy. But my present situation . . . I've gone from indenture to captivity to a miserable arranged marriage. Then I had a taste of freedom, though I felt

I owed the Jewetts whatever labor I could give them. And now marriage."

"But marriage to a good man is not a bad thing," Sarah said. "I myself find it pleasant."

Jane sighed. "Sarah, keeping house for Charles is child's play. He's never in it, and his possessions are so few it's impossible to make a mess. He's out working all day, wearing himself out, and leaves me in there with nothing to do but tend the fire and cook a little. If I had a spinning wheel or a loom . . . but I can't ask him for that because he has no money, and that is my fault. I'd like to do something to help him pay off the debt and get ahead with the farm, the way he wants to."

"Give it time, dear. You're only just married."

"I know."

Jane bowed over her handwork. It was true her heart was restless. She felt she was a disappointment to her husband. But there were other things she couldn't express, to Sarah or to Charles.

"Surely you can find something else to put your hand to."

"I do. I bake and I sew, but I'm running out of flour and material. I hate to ask him for anything, after he gave every penny he had for me. Perhaps in the fall, when our crops are in, I can do something that will bring in money. Would you keep me in prayer, Sarah?"

"Of course. In fact, we can pray together right now." Sarah laid aside her knitting and leaned toward her friend.

Jane was taken aback at first. She felt the rush of tears flooding her eyes. "Thank you. I fear I haven't prayed enough. I do want to please Charles. I'm just not sure I know how."

"Then we shall ask that God will show you."

The next evening, when Charles came to supper, he found Jane flitting about the cabin. The table was set, and she seemed to have cooked more dishes than usual. She'd stewed the rabbit he'd brought her that morning but also fixed pumpkin and biscuits and a spicy-smelling tart.

He tried to recall what Richard had told him as he went to the worktable. She had filled the washbowl with warm water for him and laid out a linen towel. "It smells delicious," he ventured, feeling a bit silly.

"Thank you."

Her warm response encouraged him. "Dried apple tart, is it?"

"Yes. Do you like it?"

"I'm sure I shall."

They sat down together, but still she seemed livelier, more eager than usual.

After asking the blessing, Charles mentally went over the bleak conversation with Richard again. "And how was your day? Do you have everything you need about the house?"

"Well . . . the flour is running a bit short." She peered at him almost timidly.

"I'm sure I can get some on credit from the trader."

Jane hesitated then said, "Sarah gave me more yarn yesterday, and I've started a new pair of socks for you."

He served out the stew, and they ate in silence. Jane kept looking at him across the table. He wondered if something had happened that he didn't know about.

After a few minutes she said, "Charles, I thought of a plan to help you earn the money back."

He winced. Apparently she persisted in thinking about his debt. He wished she would leave it be. He would earn the money and repay Richard and his father, and that would be that.

"I think we'll be fine," he murmured. "Don't trouble yourself over it."

"But I can help you — I'm sure of it."

He looked closely at her earnest face. Even though this was not the topic he would have chosen, she seemed more eager to talk than she had ever been with him.

"All right, then, what is your plan?"

"We could open our home to travelers."

He stared at her. "What?"

"Think of it! We'll have plenty of space with the new room you are building, and the village has no inn. There's only the ordinary. Ladies who travel don't like to stay at a tavern. But we could offer a quiet place and good food. Folks who come to Cochecho on business or who need a place to stay while building a house could stay here."

As he listened, Charles felt his world tilting. Strangers in the cabin? Let his wife cook and wash for peddlers and such?

"What do you think?"

Her gray eyes reflected the firelight, and he hated to dash her hopes. He allowed himself a brief moment to consider accepting her plan. Would it be so bad?

Yes, it certainly would.

He cleared his throat. "It's true I haven't much ready cash just now, but our farm will supply most of our needs, and I truly believe my late-season furs will fetch nearly enough to square things with the Dudleys. By harvesttime . . ."

Her face fell. "You don't like my idea."

He hesitated. "Well, it has merit, I'm sure, but . . . actually I see no need to earn money in this manner. It would only make more work for us both, and . . . and it would bring strangers into our home."

She blinked at him, frowning. "I only wish to help, Husband."

"Of course. And I thank you. But you know, my dear, you don't even like to go to the trading post around strangers. I'm surprised you would want to open our private home like that."

"It wouldn't be the ideal, but if it would pay off our debt . . ."

"Let me handle that, please." He looked deep into her eyes. "Please."

She looked away first. "As you wish."

Charles reached for another biscuit. The atmosphere in the room had changed. Jane's features drooped, and she kept her eyes lowered. He tried to think how he could make things better without giving in to her suggestion. While he'd told himself — and Richard, for that matter — he would do anything to make Jane happy, this was beyond anything he had imagined she would want.

Her fork clicked against her pewter plate as she laid it down. "Would you like tea?"

139

Her voice was stilted. He had hurt her feelings.

Charles forced a smile. "I should like that very much, thank you."

She rose and went to the hearth. He racked his brain for a way to keep her from closing up on him again. If they could keep talking, perhaps they could unravel this unpleasant incident and start fresh. Back to her excitement and eagerness. She'd worked extra hard to prepare a special meal for him; he knew she had. She'd set the scene before she presented her plan to him. And now he had shattered her hopes.

"Jane, please don't take me wrong. I do appreciate your willingness to help me out. I just think . . . Well, we live far from the village, for one thing. Travelers won't want to come all the way out here for a bed. And you might find yourself overwhelmed with work."

"I'm strong, Charles. I can work hard."

"Yes, but what if . . . what if you found yourself in a . . . a delicate condition, and you had to serve people anyway?" He felt his face grow scarlet at mentioning the possibility.

Jane stopped with her back to him and didn't move for several seconds.

He gulped air. *Now I've done it. How would*

you get out of this, Richard?

Jane turned slowly with his cup in her hands. "What if I can't?"

"Can't what?"

"What if I can't have children, Charles?"

Her words silenced him as nothing else could. He realized he was staring at her and made himself look away. He picked up his knife and laid it down again. They'd only been married a couple of weeks, and she was talking about possibly never having children. Was there something he didn't know? He'd always imagined he would have sons. Was she telling him she couldn't bear children? Maybe they should have put the marriage off until they knew each other better and felt more comfortable in each other's presence. For the first time, he now wondered if he had chosen the wrong mate.

She brought the tea over and placed it on the table at his elbow; then she turned away and poured dishwater into her basin.

Charles couldn't think of a single word to say.

EIGHT

When Jane rose the next morning, her husband had already left the house. She dressed quickly and put water and parched corn in a kettle over the fire; then she opened the door.

The temperature had moderated, and a steady *thunk-thunk* met her ears. Although the sun was not yet above the trees, Charles was already chopping away. Probably he was shaping the logs he would use to build the new room on the house.

He had his own well-ordered plans. Jane felt selfish for suggesting a different course that would add to his labor. He was doing something nice for her. Having a bedchamber would be nice. Their clothing and personal items would be out of sight when visitors came. Many colonists lived out their lives in one-room cottages, but Charles had bigger ideas.

She hurried back to her worktable, determined to present him in an hour with a breakfast that would fill him up with tasty food and strengthen him for a full morning's work. As she worked, she prayed for wisdom.

When all was ready, she went out to call her husband to come in and eat. She found him behind the house, shaping the end of a log that would fit with another to make a corner joint. The new room would perfectly match the cabin, a sturdy, graceful addition that seemed a part of the original, she was sure. Charles would not build anything that was not both beautiful and functional. She wanted to tell him that she knew this about him.

Before she could speak, movement on the path that came through the woods from the Dudleys' house caught her eye.

Ben Jewett trotted toward them.

"Charles," she said.

He lowered his ax and looked at her.

Jane pointed toward the boy.

Charles straightened. "Ben! What's the matter?"

Jane knew Charles was thinking the same as she — Ben wouldn't come so far this early unless with an urgent message.

The boy arrived panting and stood for a moment to catch his breath. "My mother.

She's ill. Joseph and Abby, too. Father wishes Miss Jane to come if she is able."

"Of course I'll come," Jane said. "Did you break your fast, Ben?"

"Nay."

"I've food ready, and Goodman Gardner and I were about to sit down to eat. Won't you join us? Then I will gather a few things and come."

Ben pulled in another deep breath. "Father says hurry. He and Christine are doing all they can. He wanted to take Ruth, Constance, and John to the Heards', but they wouldn't have 'em."

"Why not?" Charles asked sharply.

"Smallpox."

Charles stared at Jane. "You can't —"

"Of course I can, Charles. I must."

"Nay. You are my wife, and I say you can't."

Jane glared at him. Just when she was softening and preparing to apologize for her selfishness, he would decide to bully her.

Charles breathed heavily, eyeing her with open disapproval. "Jane, I don't wish you to go into the sickness."

"But the Jewetts were so kind to me. No one else would take me in last year, but they showed true charity. I cannot refuse to go to Elizabeth now, Charles."

144

He stood still, his mouth set and his dark eyes narrowed.

"Come," she said, including Ben in her invitation. "Let us pray and eat together."

Charles offered the blessing for their meal and a heartfelt petition for the Jewett family. They began to eat in silence. Jane started to speak once but felt it best to hold her remarks.

When she had finished her portion, she rose and refilled the men's plates. Then she began to tidy her work area. She didn't have much to take with her that would help her patients, but she could offer her hard work. She tucked her extra shift, apron, and sewing kit into a basket.

When she fetched her cloak, Charles stood and watched her, his face set in displeasure. She pulled her shawl about her shoulders and over her hair before she met his gaze. "I must go to them."

A muscle in his cheek twitched. "Ben should stay here."

The boy looked up at him, his mouth open.

"What if he is already carrying the disease?" Jane asked.

"Then I am already exposed. If he takes ill, I'll bring him to the parsonage, and we shall all suffer together."

"Father told me to come back with Goody Gardner or Goody Dudley, whichever would come," Ben said.

"You stopped at the Dudleys'?" Charles asked.

"At Richard Dudley's. Goodman Richard wouldn't let me enter his house."

Charles frowned. "That's not like him."

"Perhaps it is for Sarah's sake," Jane suggested. Charles grimaced, and she looked away. Richard was protecting Sarah, but she wouldn't let Charles protect her. Again she had failed to meet his standard of what a wife should be.

As she left the house with Ben, she felt Charles's bleak stare. She did not look back for fear she would lose her resolve.

Charles watched Jane go and felt helpless. What if she never came back? What if she decided she preferred the swarming Jewett household to the coldness between them? Worse yet, what if she caught smallpox and died?

Dear God, how could things go so wrong in such a short time?

He sat down hard on the bench at the table. The food she had prepared for him so skillfully still cooled on his plate. He looked around. She had taken all of her things, or nearly all. What if this bereavement was permanent? Already he was lonely, and she'd been gone three minutes. She had to return. He couldn't stand to go back to being a single man, living alone. He knew things could be better for him and Jane. They had to be.

Lord, please bring us through this. Show us how to work together in harness to honor You and build a godly home together. Please, Father, bring her back to me.

The next day, Jane dressed Constance in her warmest clothing and prepared to walk with her and ten-year-old John to Goody Deane's cottage. Across the village, several families had been stricken with the sickness, and most quarantined themselves, refusing to open their doors to outsiders. The meetinghouse had remained closed on Sunday, and no services were held. But the widow had come across the road that morning and stridently told the parson to get whatever of his young ones were still healthy out of there and take them to her house.

Distraught at his wife's failing condition and the new baby's listlessness, the pastor agreed. Ruth, the toddler, had also presented a rash that morning and lay whimpering next to her mother on the pallet.

Elizabeth lay flushed with fever, angry red spots marking her usually clear complexion, and the little baby labored with every breath. Abby, the seven-year-old, was fretful but still active. Christine had placed her on a straw tick near the hearth and given the loft over to the as-yet healthy boys. Abby seemed less ill than the others, and Jane had wrapped her hands in linen to keep her from scratching her pox.

"Do you wish the children to bid their mother good-bye ere I take them to Goody Deane?" she asked the pastor.

The Reverend Jewett looked up at her with dull eyes. "Nay. Bring them not near her. I know it is hard for them, but the old woman is right. Keeping them away may save their lives. Ben, you go, too. If I have need of you, I will fetch you."

"But, Father —"

"Nay, son, do not oppose me now. Go and help to occupy your brother and sister. If there is aught you can do for Goody Deane, then put your hand to it. Fetch wood and water for her, or whatever else she can find for you to do."

Constance began to cry, and Jane scooped her up in her arms.

Ben scowled but grabbed his coat and followed her and John out the door.

When she had safely deposited the three children at the widow's, Jane returned to the parsonage.

Christine was pouring water into the washtub. The parson still sat by Elizabeth's head, patting her brow with a damp cloth.

"Shall I bathe Ruth and Joseph again?" Jane asked Christine.

"Aye. I thought to put fresh linen on the bed and wash the soiled things."

Jane nodded and went about her grim tasks. An hour later she fixed corn pone and pumpkin sauce for dinner.

"Come, Pastor, you must eat and keep up your strength."

Christine set a cup of cider on the table for him. "Aye, you mustn't wear yourself out. Elizabeth and the children will need you."

He sighed and rose, stretching his long arms. "Is it Monday?"

"Tuesday, sir," Jane replied.

"I don't know how to thank you girls. When this is over, if you haven't succumbed . . ."

"Don't think of that now, sir. Just pray. The Lord has given us strength so far, and we are thankful we can help you." Jane handed him a small pot of preserves. She remembered making them last summer with

Elizabeth, after she and Sarah and Christine had taken all the children out to pick blueberries.

Elizabeth moaned, and Jane hurried to her side just in time to hold a wooden bowl for her while she retched. Elizabeth lay back exhausted, and Jane rinsed a cloth and wiped her face. Her skin felt hot.

"There, dear. Rest now," Jane whispered.

Elizabeth sighed. "I don't know how I can heave when I've nothing in my stomach but a few spoonfuls of water my husband gave me."

"Easy. Let the sickness take its course."

Elizabeth's dark eyes focused on her face. "Jane."

"Aye, 'tis me."

"You should be at home with Charles."

"When you are better. Don't fret about him. He is used to fending for himself."

"You must love him, dear Jane. Do all you can to help him. Charles is a good man."

"Aye, he is that."

"Treat him kindly. He needs you, you know. Show him all your heart."

Jane nodded, not certain how she could do that. But she would not trouble Elizabeth with her turmoil. "I shall try."

Elizabeth's gaze darted about the room. "Samuel?"

"Here, my love!" The pastor leaped from his bench.

Jane quickly moved out of his way and took the slop bowl out to the garden behind the house. She hadn't paused for her shawl, and she shivered. Spring would come grudgingly in this harsh territory.

When she entered the house again, Christine drew her aside. "The baby is gone."

Jane gasped. "No!"

"Aye. But Goody Jewett knows it not. Her husband handed the little one to me and bid me place him on the chair. He says he will tend to him when his wife's crisis is past."

"Have you hope for Elizabeth?"

Christine lowered her eyes and shook her head slightly. "I doubt she is long for this world."

Jane threw herself into the drudgery of caring for the sick. She and Christine did all within their power to keep the invalids comfortable and the house spotless, but to no avail. Two hours later, Elizabeth Jewett breathed her last with her husband at her side. Jane's desolation nearly overwhelmed her, but she and Christine continued to care for Abby and Ruth, who seemed no worse as the day passed.

The parson went next door to break it to

the other children that their mother was dead. He told Jane not to expect him home soon, as he must walk to the ordinary to find someone to build a coffin while she and Christine bathed the bodies of the mother and baby and dressed them in fresh clothing.

Jane thought her heart would break as they performed the tasks, but harder still was holding Ruth and Abby after their father returned and told them the news. Their sobs wrenched her, and Jane's tears mingled with theirs.

Later that day, the bodies were removed to a disused shed near the mill, to be stored there until the ground should thaw. The pastor sent Jane and Christine up to the loft in the evening, saying he would watch over Abby and Ruth and they must sleep.

Jane looked down at him from the top of the ladder. He sat hunched in the chair by the hearth, as still as a statue.

The next morning, the pastor staggered when he rose from the breakfast table. Jane seized his arm.

"Steady, sir. You must lie down."

The pastor stared at her with glassy eyes. Jane prayed he suffered only exhaustion. He rested a few hours but then insisted on rising again to help care for his daughters. By evening he was as feverish as little Ruth, though Abby seemed to be gaining strength. At Christine's insistence, he tumbled into bed once more.

Jane and Christine sat down at the table together for a bite of supper. All three patients slept fitfully for the moment.

"We must take turnabout nursing them tonight," Christine said.

Jane nodded. "And I think we should bring Ben over to tend his father."

"But what if Ben takes ill?" Christine's eyes filled with tears. "We mustn't let any more of the children into this. If the pastor survives, we don't want to see him bury any more of his kin."

"I know, but . . ." Jane looked over at the pallet where the big man lay. It would be difficult for the two young women to care for him properly, and propriety was another question. She looked at Christine again and saw beads of sweat standing on her friend's brow, yet the room was chilly.

"Christine, be you ill?"

"Nay, I'm tired, is all."

"Are you sure?"

Christine pushed away from the table. "Aye. But if you'll take the first watch tonight, I shall lie down for a bit." She stood and clutched the edge of the table. Jane saw her shudder, and then Christine sat down again.

"You *are* ill." Jane rushed around the table. "Come, let us remove your skirt and stays. Lie down with Abby."

"Nay, I can go to the loft."

"I shan't let you climb the ladder, shaking as you are." Jane supported her as they hobbled across the room toward Abby's pallet.

It took her half an hour to help Christine undress and situate her for the night. Before they were done, Christine began to shake with chills, and Jane scrambled to the loft for extra blankets.

As she descended the ladder, the pastor moaned and turned over, groping for the slop bowl.

God, help me! I cannot nurse four people alone.

A knock sounded at the door. Jane set the blankets on the table and hurried across the room. She was surprised that anyone would come near a house known to be infected with smallpox. When she raised the latch and opened the door, she caught her breath. Never had an answered prayer looked so good to her. "Charles!"

"Aye, I'm here. I heard Goody Jewett

is dead."

" 'Tis true, and now her husband has sickened. Christine, as well. Oh, Charles, I'm so glad to see you." Tears flooded her eyes. "I don't want you to get sick, but I need help."

He stepped inside and shut the door. "I've brought you a rabbit so you can make some broth. Tell me what to do, and then get some rest."

She sobbed and put her hands to her face. The next instant she felt his strong arms about her. She couldn't stop her weeping, but Charles held her with her face against his cold woolen coat, stroking her hair. For a moment she let herself lean against him and feel his strength and support. God had speedily answered her prayer.

At last she took a deep breath and straightened. "I'm so glad you came."

He touched her cheek. "So am I. And I shall stay with you as long as there is need."

NINE

April blew in wet and gray. The snow in the village street melted, and the ground beneath it oozed with mud. Jane and Charles worked side by side. They hardly stepped outside the little parsonage for nearly a week except for wood and water or to empty the slop bowls.

One morning when Charles came in with two buckets of water, he told Jane the river was clear of ice. "The snow is nearly gone, and the breeze is warm."

The patients had passed the feverish, nauseous stage of the disease and seemed likely to recover. After their rashes appeared, Jane knew they would be weak and uncomfortable for several weeks. Abby, however, seemed much better by this time, though she still rubbed at her scabs and fussed about the itching.

News began to trickle in from the community. Charles exchanged greetings with others when he went for water, spreading the word that the pastor was still very ill but likely to survive.

On Sunday morning, a service was held for the few who came out, with one of the deacons leading a time of scripture reading and prayer for the sick.

Because of their close association with the patients, Jane and Charles stayed away, lest they even now begin to show signs of disease and spread it to others. But Charles stood in the front yard when the meeting was over and gathered news from all who passed.

The Dudleys were spared, but Heards' garrison was hit hard, and three had died there. A fisherman and his wife both died, and the trader's son was ill and not apt to recover.

As the patients at the parsonage improved, Jane spent less time cleaning and laundering and more time baking, for Abby's appetite had returned, and Ruth began to eat solid food again. Several of the parishioners brought gifts of food to the parsonage door. Jane shared this bounty with Goody Deane, who still kept the three healthy children.

Late one evening, Charles took Jane's arm and steered her gently into Elizabeth Jewett's chair. He sat down on one of the benches by the table and faced her.

"I shall leave you in the morning, if you think you can manage now."

The thought of his going saddened her, but she realized he had left much undone at home while helping her. "All shall be well here now, I think. Thank you for coming and for working so hard with me."

"Aye, well, don't bring the other children home until all your patients have lost their scabs."

Jane nodded. This advice had been given by the parson himself before he took ill. "I fear Ben and John have tired of living with the Widow Deane."

"So do I. I walked over this evening and told the boys they could go home with me in the morning if they wished. They can help me and Richard get on with the new room we're building."

"If you wish to take them, I'm sure it would be a help. Pastor is starting to fret about them and fears they'll wear out the old woman with their restlessness."

Charles's dark eyes were fixed upon her, and Jane wondered what he was thinking. In the past ten days, she'd had little time to meditate on the advice Elizabeth had given her. "Love him," her friend had said. How did a woman go about that? Jane was still not sure she knew how to love her husband. But she had a new conviction that she wanted to.

He reached out and touched her hand with his warm fingers. "When you are ready, send me word, and I will come for you."

"All right."

He nodded. "Get some rest, then. I'll wake you in a few hours, and I'll sleep until dawn."

Jane rested better that night than she had in a long time, though the lumpy straw tick in the loft was uncomfortable. She woke when he came and touched her shoulder gently. In the near darkness, she pulled on her overskirt, stays, and bodice. By the time she found her shoes, Charles had taken her place in bed and was breathing softly.

He came down from the loft at first light without her calling him. After he stoked the fire and filled her wood box and water pails, she fed him well on the plain fare the parsonage afforded.

Christine and the pastor were stirring as he donned his coat and picked up his musket. "Step outside with me, Jane."

She took her shawl from its peg and followed him onto the doorstone.

Charles took her chin in his hand, turning her face up toward his. "I know it might be a couple more weeks, but . . . you will come home?"

"Aye."

He smiled then, and his features softened. He stooped and kissed her softly then stepped back.

Jane watched him stride across the street toward Goody Deane's cottage. Warmth flooded her.

Dear Lord, are You answering my prayer? Because I think I am beginning to love him. Thank You.

Charles turned in the street and looked back at her.

Jane waved, and he lifted his hat with a tired grin before approaching the widow's door.

Two weeks later, Jane helped Christine to dress, and they fixed breakfast together. Abby seemed as healthy as she had ever been, with only a couple of dark scars on her cheeks revealing her prolonged illness.

The pastor came to the table for the first time in weeks. "I'm still a bit shaky, but I believe I shall stand in the pulpit this Sunday." He sank onto the bench and sighed.

Jane poured his cup full of hot tea. "Give yourself time to recover, sir," she counseled.

After he said the blessing, Jane brought a kettle of corn mush from the fire and ladled out the portions for the others. "Here, Abby. Goodman Dudley brought some nice milk yesterday. Have some on your samp. And there's a bit of maple sugar Mrs. Otis sent over."

Abby wriggled in anticipation. "Can Connie come home today?"

"Not yet, child," her father said. "Your scabs are gone, but Ruth and I are still peppered, and Miss Christine is not quite well yet."

"I feel stronger each day," Christine said. "Before you know it, Abby, you'll be helping me do the Monday washing."

Abby smiled up at her, but suddenly the little girl's face crumpled. "I miss Mama."

The pastor said nothing, but he looked as though he might cry, too.

Jane slipped her arm around Abby's shoulders and pulled her close. "We all miss her sorely. I shall never forget how kind your mother was to me."

"Nor I," Christine said. "She was a dear friend, and a blessing to many."

The pastor pushed back from the table. "Forgive me, ladies, but I feel the need for some fresh air."

Jane eyed him warily, knowing his full

strength would not return for some time. "Do you need company, sir?"

"Nay. I shall not be long."

He paused briefly at the door to take his coat from a peg then hurried outside.

Tears bathed Abby's face as she stared at the closed door. "Will Papa die?"

"Nay, child," said Christine. "He is getting well, as are you and I. Ruthie, too."

As though she had heard her name, the two-year-old let out a wail. Jane jumped up and hastened to her pallet. "Well now, Ruth, are you hungry? I thought you would sleep the morning away." Quickly she changed the little girl's clothes and carried her to the table, where she sat down with Ruth on her lap.

Christine, meanwhile, had risen and brought a fresh portion of samp to the table.

Jane dipped a spoonful of the cooked corn dish and held it to the little girl's mouth.

Ruth pushed the spoon away and burrowed against Jane's bodice. "Mama! I want Mama."

Abby's tears began to flow again, and both girls sobbed.

"Oh dear," said Christine. "What shall we do?" Her own eyes glistened.

Jane pulled in a deep breath. "I suppose we shall all cry together, and many times before we are through." A firm knock sounded at the door, and she rose to answer it.

Charles stood outside carrying a burlap sack. "Good day." His somber brown eyes searched Jane's face. "I've brought the boys back."

She looked past him toward the muddy street. "Where are they?"

"We met the parson in the dooryard, and they've walked out back with him." Charles shook his head. "He looks to have lost half his flesh."

"Aye. They're all thin. It's only by God's grace they survived."

"All are gaining strength now?"

She nodded. "Did the boys wear you out?"

"Nay, they're good boys. They helped me a lot, and you shall see the results of their labor when you come home. But they were restless, wanting news of their father. I had them bring their stuff and told them they could stay if he allowed it."

"I expect he will. He misses having them all about him now that he's up again. And the house seems very empty without his wife." Jane stepped back. "Won't you come in?"

"Yes, I'll wait to see what he says about the boys." Charles pulled his hat off and ducked beneath the lintel, blinking in the semidarkness. "What of you, Jane? Are you well? You look thin, too."

"I'm fine. A bit tired."

"I should think so."

Still at the table, Christine stood. "How good of you to come, Goodman Gardner."

"Oh, please. Call me Charles."

She nodded.

"I trust you are on the road to recovery?" he asked.

"I believe I am," Christine said.

Charles held the sack up. "I've not had much success hunting lately, but James Dudley butchered a yearling ram. He sent a hindquarter for the parsonage."

"Wonderful." Jane took the heavy sack and carried it to the worktable. "We haven't had meat here in a week. I'll make a nice soup for tonight's supper."

Charles turned his hat about in his hands. "I hoped you might come home with me, Jane."

She turned and eyed him anxiously. "I daren't leave yet, Charles. Christine is too weak to lift Ruth yet, and if the boys stay, I suppose Constance will come home, too."

He nodded at the obvious implications. More people to cook for, more washing and scrubbing. "When you are able, then."

"I shall."

"It won't be long, sir," Christine said. "You've been most kind to let us have Jane so long."

"Well, I . . ." Charles looked everywhere but at his wife. "You needed her," he said at last, crumpling his hat in his clenched hands. "This were her home for many months, and you needed her."

"Charles! Charles!"

The door crashed open, and Ben Jewett catapulted inside. Jane almost scolded him for speaking so familiarly to Goodman Gardner, but she checked herself. Charles showed no annoyance, and they had just lived two weeks together. Besides, Ben stood only a couple of inches shorter than Charles now, and no doubt he was finding his way into manhood. Perhaps Charles's acceptance and friendship would ease the way for him.

"Father says John and I may stay," Ben said, his eyes gleaming. "We are to take over all the heavy chores, and Miss Jane may go home with you."

"Nay," Jane said quickly. "I shall stay a bit longer, until your father and Christine are stronger. But we are making good progress, and we shall be glad to have you and John here to haul the water and wood."

Charles looked at her and nodded slowly. "That's right. A few more days, perhaps. She must stay. And when you don't need her anymore, then my wife shall come home."

The steady spring rains took the last of the snow and mired the village so that walking to the meetinghouse taxed the most patient souls. But only three days after the boys and Constance returned, the sun shone and the wind blew gently up from the river.

Christine urged Jane to go back to her husband. "You've been away from home a month. Charles needs you more than we do now."

Jane put her hands on her hips and surveyed the cluttered work area. "I don't know, Christine. You're not fully recovered yet. This large brood is a handful."

"Nonsense. Even Ruth is getting about again, and the pastor is back to his preaching. I've two strong boys to help me with the chores, and Goody Deane comes over every day to help me watch the girls and bake."

Jane nodded, knowing it was true. The old widow across the way seemed happy to take part in the household's recovery, and Christine made sure she went home each day with a portion of the baking. The arrangement would benefit both households.

"All right, then. I suppose you're correct." Jane pulled at the strings of her apron and took it off, rolling it into a small bundle. She went to the corner and tucked the apron into her basket with her sewing kit and extra shift. The thought of going back to the farm at the edge of the forest seemed odd. *That's my home,* she reminded herself.

"Take Ben with you," Christine said.

Jane considered that. "He would be all-over mud when he returned, and that would be more work for you. I shall be fine. The savages will wait for better travel conditions before they bother us again."

Abby and Constance stared at her. "You're leaving?" Abby wailed.

Jane went to her and embraced her and Constance. Ruth toddled to them and wriggled into the hug, too.

"I shall come again soon." Jane kissed each one's shining hair. She and Christine had bathed all the girls the day before and combed out their tangled tresses. "You must be good and help your papa and Miss Christine."

"We will." Constance's lips trembled.

"Will you come for —" Abby stopped, and tears trickled down her cheeks.

"What, dear?"

"For when they bury Mama and Baby Joseph? Papa says it won't be many weeks now."

Jane pulled her close. "Aye. Send Ben with word when the service will be held. Goodman Gardner and I will be there."

Ruth clung to her with her arms locked about Jane's neck.

Jane held her for a long moment then gently disentangled the little girl's arms. "I'll see you at meeting anyway. That's only four days away, if we're able to get there."

"The streets are so sloppy," Christine said.

"Aye, but we'll manage, unless it rains violently." Jane passed Ruth to her and looked about the little house once more. "I'll stop at the meetinghouse a moment and tell Pastor and the boys I am going."

Charles worked steadily across the back roof, adding course after course of shingles. The new room he and Richard had built was actually two and doubled the size of his house. A roomy pantry nestled between the original cabin and the spacious new bedchamber.

Not only that, but with help from John and Ben Jewett, Charles had built a clothespress. That and the rope bed were the only furnishings in the new room and left it looking bare. But he knew what he would tell Jane. There was plenty of room in there for a spinning wheel and a loom. After harvest next fall, when the cold weather came again, he would build her a loom. He thought he could copy Sarah's. And if he couldn't trade for a wheel, he'd figure out how to build that, too. His hands seemed to have a way when it came to working with wood.

And Jane, he was sure, would find other ways to brighten the room. She was clever with a needle. Maybe she could make some rugs and curtains like Sarah had in her cozy house.

If Jane came back.

The wind had a cold edge. He turned his collar up and tried to drive away the dark thoughts that crept at the edge of his mind. She'd assured him only a few days ago that she would return, and he would cling to the promise.

He reached for another shingle and saw that he'd used nearly all that he'd brought up to the roof in a bushel basket. He would have to go down for more soon. A snowflake landed on his sleeve, and he looked up. The sky had clouded over and a halfhearted, late-season snow was falling. Taking the next shingle, he laid it in place and held the nail to it. Would winter never end? If the snow thickened, he'd have to stop work.

She might want to stay and keep house at the parsonage and never come home.

He cast that thought aside and concentrated on the task at hand. A soft thump came from below, just as he was about to strike with the hammer. He hit his thumb and jumped, pulling his hand up to his mouth. His sudden movement almost overbalanced him, and fear shot through him for an instant as he wobbled on his perch.

Don't do anything suddenly on a roof, you fool, he told himself.

He sat still for a moment and took a deep breath. Suddenly he froze. He had definitely heard a muted sound. Someone was in the house.

Several thoughts ran through his mind. Indians, rifling his foodstuffs? Or Richard, come calling? A scraping sound reached him, and the stone chimney belched a big puff of smoke.

Charles smiled. Could it be? He didn't dare hope, and yet . . . Richard wouldn't build up his fire. He'd have heard him pounding and come around back first thing. Indians would steal what they could and get out. Anyone else would have knocked. It had to be Jane!

With care, he held the last shingle in place and drove the nail in. Cautiously he stood up on the board he'd temporarily fixed along the side of the roof for a brace and walked along it to the edge of the roof, where his rough ladder stood. He put his hammer in the basket and tossed it down to the ground then swung over to the ladder.

He put his tools away in the barn before going to the house door. The few minutes tortured him sweetly. His disappointment would hit hard if he was wrong. He stood in the barn doorway for half a minute, staring across the yard at the cabin.

She wouldn't have come all the way out here alone, would she? Only last summer, the congregation at another village was ambushed while leaving its Sunday meeting. Jane well knew the dangers of walking about alone and unarmed.

He sniffed the sharp breeze. Someone was cooking dried apple tart in his house.

Charles smiled and strode toward the door.

Ten

Charles closed the door loudly enough so there was no doubt Jane heard it. He removed his coat and hat and hung them near the door.

She stayed bent over her kettle at the hearth, stirring what he assumed was to be their dinner.

"Welcome home."

She turned toward him and nodded soberly; then she went to her worktable and measured some rye flour into a crockery bowl.

Charles took off his boots and hesitated. Should he speak again? Or let her go about her silent routine? "How be the Jewetts?"

"All gaining."

"The boys are pitching in?"

"Aye." She frowned over her concoction and added a teaspoon of something white. "Ben says thank ye for having them and he'll come when you plant."

"Good. I can use him." Charles carried his boots nearer the fireplace, but not too near, to dry out. The fire had burned down to coals. He nearly threw a log on, but perhaps Jane didn't want him to. "Do you be using these coals?"

"Aye."

He took a piece of oak down from the mantel and drew his knife; then he sat down on a stool beside the hearth.

Jane eyed the stick in his hand but went back to her work without speaking.

Charles couldn't help drawing an unfavorable comparison to Sarah Dudley. If Richard sat down to carve on a piece of wood, Sarah would ask him what it was. Richard would probably tease her and make her guess, but Sarah would badger him playfully until he told her. Not Jane.

Ask me. Let me tell you it's for your loom, sweet wife. Please ask me.

Five minutes later, Jane carried her Dutch oven to the hearth. She took down the small shovel, pulled a bed of red coals onto the stone hearth, and positioned the oven precisely over it. Then she scooped hot coals onto the lid. She straightened and hung up the shovel. "We shall eat soon. I'm sorry I didn't have it ready when you stopped work."

"Nay, I stopped because of the snow. And . . . I'm pleased to find you home, Jane."

She seemed to mull that over for a few seconds; then her lips twitched, but she said nothing. She returned his gaze.

He wished he could smooth out the fine crease between her eyebrows. "Have you seen the new chambers?"

She blinked. "Nay, not yet."

Charles rose and put the oak stick and his knife on the mantel. "Come, then."

He'd kept the doors to the bedchamber and pantry closed to conserve heat. Though he'd moved the bed into the new room, he had yet to sleep in there. Instead, he had thrown his pallet down near the fire the last two nights, unwilling to claim the new room as his own. He had built it for Jane. Let her decide.

She'd been away so long, he was no longer sure she would welcome him again into her bed. They'd spent far more of their short marriage apart than together, and perhaps she preferred it that way. She didn't seem any too pleased to be back here with him.

He walked to the pantry and paused, waiting for her to step over near him.

When he opened the door, she gasped. "Oh, Charles."

He let her pass him, and she stepped inside then stood gaping at the shelves he had fitted. A long board at waist height held her kneading trough and dishpan. "You did all this while I was gone?"

"Aye. Richard and his father helped me, and then Ben and John."

"I didn't expect anything so fine." Her gray eyes glittered in the dim light afforded by the one narrow window at the end of the pantry.

Charles felt a knot in his shoulders come loose, and he leaned against the door frame. She had smiled — just a little smile, but it was enough. "I'm glad you like it. When I sell my furs, I'll bring you some supplies. And at harvesttime, we'll fill these shelves."

She nodded.

He turned away and waited for her to come out.

She stepped into the main room and carefully shut the door, testing the latch.

What would she think of the new bedchamber? He wished suddenly that he'd gone to the trader and taken credit for more furniture. But no, that would only upset her again, and she'd be scheming to earn money for his increased debts. Best to pay things down slowly as he'd been doing and get the things that would make them comfortable when they could afford them.

He swung the door open. Her skirt brushed against him as she entered the room. She stood in silence so long that he walked around her and studied her face.

"It's so large," she said softly.

"Aye."

She walked to one of the windows and looked out at the woods behind the cabin.

"We can put up the shutters inside to keep the cold out," he said. No need to mention that the shutters would also keep the Indians from firing into the house. "The fireplace isn't as large as the other one, but it will take the chill off at night. And I . . . I thought you'd want your loom and wheel in here later." Still she said nothing. "Or we could partition it off separate, if you'd like that. But I thought you might like to keep it one large room."

"I can make rugs," she said.

His relief was so great, he almost laughed.

"Aye, and curtains if you like."

She nodded, and he grinned.

"It's a fine room." She turned slowly, and her gaze fixed on the new clothespress. She threw him a look that was almost inquisitive, and his pulse quickened. Slowly she approached it and opened the doors.

He was glad he hadn't put anything in it

yet. "You can arrange your things however you like. Oh, and Sarah sent this over for you." He went to the bed and lifted two lengths of material he had left folded there.

"What is it?"

"Some worsted and flannel. Richard's father took a boat to Boston and came back with a lot of stuff for his wife and Catherine and Sarah. Too much stuff, Sarah said."

Jane nodded. Sarah loved to give simple gifts, now that she was able. "That's kind of them."

He laid the cloth down and stepped away.

Jane reached out and felt it.

Charles renewed his resolve to take their marriage at her pace. Jane was his wife until death should part them — that much he had settled with God. He would do all he could to make a go of it. Even if that meant keeping his distance.

He pulled in a deep breath. "Jane?"

She looked toward him, a question in her eyes.

"I . . . well, I thought if you . . . if you preferred it, I could stay out yonder." He jerked his head toward the main room.

"For what?"

"I mean . . . I could sleep out there if you want me to."

Her features froze.

Charles felt suddenly empty. He leaned against the stone fireplace and waited for her to say something — anything.

Instead, she turned to look out the second window.

"Jane?"

She didn't turn.

He sighed. "I'll bring some wood in here and make up a fire so it will be warm if you wish to work in here this afternoon."

As he headed for the door, she spoke. "Charlie."

He spun around. "What?"

"We be wed."

"Aye."

She nodded. "So don't be daft." She brushed past him into the main room and began to scrub the table.

He stood in the doorway, uncertain how to take her words. Was he daft to build a fire and burn extra wood when it wasn't needed? Or to . . .

He stared at her straight back and her thin shoulders, at her dark blond hair that glinted red, pulled up on the back of her head, at the curve of her neck above the edge of her bodice.

Lord, I shall take this as a sign of hope.

In early May, the breezes wafting off the

river warmed the village. The maples, oaks, and beeches uncurled tiny leaves. And the sexton dug graves in the churchyard for those who had died during the winter.

Charles and Jane made the trip to the village.

The muddy paths were drying out, and the entire Dudley family walked with them. James and his wife, along with Catherine, Stephen, Richard, and Sarah, carried gifts for the Jewett family: parched corn, a jug of molasses, bacon, and a large sack of wool for Christine to spin.

Charles carried a cake Jane had baked and a pair of small wooden dolls he had carved for Ruth and Constance. Jane added a few scraps of flannel for the girls to use for doll clothes. Charles wasn't sure the little girls would find his dolls appealing, but Jane assured him that anything new would catch their attention for at least a short time and keep their thoughts from dwelling on their grief.

Nearly all the villagers gathered in the churchyard for the occasion. Though it saddened them to bid a last farewell to the departed, it also cheered them to stand together in the sunshine and see all who had survived the cruel winter. Parson Weaver had come all the way out from

Portsmouth to preach the funeral sermon for Elizabeth Jewett and the other smallpox victims.

Charles thought Pastor Jewett looked stronger. His step was certainly steadier, but his large frame was still too spare, and new lines etched his forehead.

After the graveside services, Jane and Charles went with the Dudleys to visit the trading post. By unspoken agreement, Charles and Jane bought nothing, but he noted the pleasure Sarah and her sister-in-law, Catherine, took in picking out notions for their sewing projects. He wished he could tell Jane to purchase whatever she liked. Someday he'd be able to do that.

She glanced toward him just then, over the tables of merchandise, and smiled. It was almost as though she'd spoken to him. *I have all I need, Husband.*

The next evening, Charles sorted his sacks of seed. Jane had traded shell beans for pumpkin seeds with Sarah.

"This be the seeds I promised Christine." She set aside a small pouch containing a selection of vegetable seeds.

Charles nodded. "We've plenty."

"She has some Goody Jewett saved, but I want her to have plenty to plant in the garden at the parsonage."

"We can take them to her Sunday."

"Thank you, Charles."

He shrugged. It was a small thing. And yet he felt that they grew closer each day, and their purposes converged as they learned to know each other better. They seemed to talk more now, though it was usually of inconsequential things.

Jane's growing contentment soothed him, and he was happier than he'd been since the day she agreed to be his wife.

Jane set off one pleasant morning toward Sarah and Richard's cabin. The men had widened the path through the woods, and from their yard Charles could see the peak of the Dudleys' roof and watch her nearly all the way to the neighbors' house. Jane was permitted to make the short walk unescorted, so long as he knew she was going. This small added freedom cheered Jane. She and Sarah made the journey one way or the other nearly every day.

In Jane's basket was a baby's gown she was stitching for Sarah. The glad news of a coming child was not unexpected. When the smallpox struck two months earlier, Jane had wondered if that were Richard's reason for not allowing his wife to go into the disease-ridden Jewett household. It gave the

181

two young women much to talk about these days.

As she came to the corner of the stockade Richard was building, she saw two smaller figures skipping about in the yard between the fence and the house. "Abby! Constance! How delightful to find you here," she called.

As the girls turned toward her, their faces lit with joy. "Miss Jane!" Abby ran to her with Constance only a step behind. "We came to call."

"What a treat." Jane embraced them both. "May I assume Miss Christine is inside?"

"And Ruthie, too," Constance said.

"Indeed! Did Ruth walk all this way with you?"

"Papa carried her," Abby told her. "He had to see Mr. James Dudley, and he said Miss Christine might as well take us for a visit to the younger Dudleys. So here we are."

The cottage door opened, and Sarah grinned at her. "I thought I heard your voice. Come in, Jane. I found some new wintergreen leaves yesterday, and we're just about to have tea."

Jane greeted Christine with enthusiasm and allowed Ruth to climb up on her lap as she sat at Sarah's table. The little girl clutched the wooden doll Charles had made her, and it was now dressed in a tiny linen shift and flannel overskirt. Jane recognized Christine's meticulous hemstitching. "What fine clothing your dolly has."

Ruth smiled and held the doll close.

Christine lifted a linen napkin from her basket on the table, disclosing a plate of small raisin cakes. The little girls' eyes grew large as she placed it on the table. "There now, young ladies, one cake apiece."

The three Jewett girls quickly claimed their treats, and Jane also accepted one of the cakes.

"Christine was just giving me the village news," Sarah said. "She is living with Goody Deane now."

"Is Goody Deane ill?" Jane asked. "Does she need your nursing?"

"Nay," said Christine. "It's for propriety."

"To quell the gossips," Sarah said in a low voice. "You know how it is in Cochecho."

"Aye," said Jane. Only the Indians inflicted more harm on the village than did the wagging tongues of its residents.

Christine leaned toward her and murmured, "One of the deacons told the pastor it was unconscionable for him to keep me at the parsonage any longer. It struck him to the heart, poor man. He's been so diligent since his dear wife died, trying to do all he can for his people and yet be at hand for the children when they need him."

Sarah clucked her tongue. "It must have shocked him to learn his people could think ill of him."

"Unfortunately, that is the way folks think," Christine said. "Now I fear he's sunk into his studies. Spends all day at the meetinghouse poring over his books, since the weather took a turn for the warmer."

"How sad. He was very fond of Elizabeth." Jane looked down at Ruth, but the little girl seemed to be concentrating on her raisin cake.

Sarah refilled her kettle and stirred up the fire. "I suppose that some folks would consider it improper for you to stay there, even with five children in the house."

"They do," Christine said.

"So you sleep at Goody Deane's across the way and go back and forth?" Jane asked.

"Aye, both of us. I think the widow enjoys it tremendously, doing for other people. She sweeps and spins and plays cat's cradle with the girls. She's good company for me, now that you two have deserted me."

Jane stared at her. "Well, Miss Hardin! I don't think I've ever heard you speak so much before."

Christine chuckled.

"Goody Deane is large on conversation," Abby Jewett said. "She doesn't believe in keeping silence all day."

A smile tugged at Christine's lips. "She says the nuns taught me that, and I must get over it."

"Perhaps she's right." Sarah sat down with them and sipped her tea.

When the three little girls had finished their refreshments, Sarah allowed them all to go out again to play.

"Stay inside the stockade. Abby, you'll watch Ruth closely? You know the fence isn't finished yet, and I don't want her wandering off."

"I will, Miss Sarah."

When Sarah rejoined the others at the table, Jane said, "Charles tells me that as soon as the men have their corn planted, they'll put up the new addition to the parsonage."

"It can't come too soon," Christine said. "Though it will be bittersweet for the pastor, I suppose. Elizabeth so looked forward to having more space. Now it will be just him and the children."

"But they need privacy for the girls, and a quiet place for the pastor to study in winter without shivering over at the meetinghouse," Jane said.

Christine nodded. "Aye. The boys will have the loft again, and they can get all the bedding out of the keeping room."

Sarah smiled. "The church folk will be able to visit the parson without stepping on quilts and babies."

They all sat in silence for a moment, remembering the little boy who was buried with Elizabeth just a few days earlier.

Jane wiped a tear from her cheek. "I do miss Elizabeth."

"Poor Pastor." Christine lifted her apron and wiped her eyes with the hem.

Sarah lifted Jane's cup to refill it with tea. "Come, let us talk of more pleasant things."

"All right," Christine said. "I've a bit of pleasant news. It means less work for me. Ruth has stopped wearing clouts."

Jane and Sarah laughed.

"That is good news," Jane said.

"Aye. I've washed them all, and on Sunday you and Richard can stop in after meeting and get them. A present for your little one."

"Oh, that is very generous," Sarah said.

"Well, the Jewetts shan't be needing them anymore, and Parson said to give them to some as can use them. Of course I thought of you, though some are worn quite thin."

"Thank you. I shall be glad to have them, but our baby won't be here until November." Sarah's face went a becoming, delicate pink. "If anyone in the village needs them before, you may pass them along."

A half hour later, the pastor came to collect Christine and the children. He greeted Jane cheerfully, but she noted the drawn look about his eyes. He invited her and Sarah to visit Christine and the children at the parsonage whenever they wished. Both promised to come soon.

"So tragic," Jane said as she and Sarah watched the figures stride down the path toward the village.

"He'll not soon leave off grieving for Elizabeth," Sarah agreed.

"She told me I must love Charles, you know, just before she died." Jane glanced over at Sarah to catch her reaction.

"Oh? And how are you doing? I've been praying for you all this time, since you told me how much you wanted to please him."

"I try. But I'm not sure I give him all he needs. He doesn't seem truly happy."

"Then you must figure out what more he needs."

Jane smiled. "I know what he *wants*. He's hinted it a couple of times."

"And what is that?"

"A child."

"And is that so impossible? Surely if I can

do it . . ."

Sarah's coy laugh almost lightened Jane's heart, but her memories squelched the possibility. "Perhaps."

"Ah. I see. Your marriage in Canada. I should have realized. Three years with Monsieur Robataille and no babies."

"Actually —" Jane bit her lip, but it was too late. She'd already snagged Sarah's attention. "Actually there was a child," she whispered.

Sarah's features drooped. "It's cold out here. Come inside and tell me about it." She drew Jane back into the house and stoked the fire once more.

Jane pulled her chair close to the hearth and kept her shawl, for the brief time outside and her dark thoughts had chilled her.

"So" — Sarah placed a fresh cup of tea in Jane's hand — "what happened?"

Jane sat for a long moment, looking into the blaze. It was something she didn't want to dredge up, but Sarah was a woman and her best friend. And she knew part of it now. Jane couldn't very well back down and refuse to confide in her.

She started to sip her tea, but it was too hot, so she set it over onto the table and folded her hands in her lap. "Monsieur Robataille was not present when it happened. He went away, you see. He always went in spring, on a long voyage. And before he left, he told me all the things I must do in his absence, just as he did the year before. I must tend the gardens and the livestock, arrange for men to get the harvest in, and so on. And if I couldn't hire men to do it, I must do it myself."

"Did he know you were expecting a child?"

"He knew." Jane bowed her head and fought the stinging sensation of tears trying to escape. "He had one hired man to tend the sheep. But the shepherd was old, and he was not able by himself to do the heavy farmwork. It was up to me to find someone. The year before I had hired three boys, and I thought we did well, but when Monsieur Robataille returned in the fall, he was not pleased. We were late getting some of the crops in, and they were past prime."

"What happened?"

Jane reached for her tea and took a drink. Still Sarah waited. Jane did not look up at her, but she said, "He struck me."

Sarah drew a deep breath. "I'm so sorry."

Jane nodded. "It was not the first time, nor the last. And so I was determined to do it right the second year. He told me that when he came back, he wanted to find the baby in the cradle and the crops in the barn."

"Charming man, wasn't he?" Sarah raised her cup to her lips.

Jane sat still, feeling the welcome heat of the fire on her face. She let her shawl slip down from her shoulders. "I couldn't get enough help, and in August I spent nearly every day in the fields. All day we worked, bringing in hay, harvesting corn. And then one morning I woke up, and I knew something wasn't right. I was bleeding, but it wasn't time for the baby until October." She sobbed. "I sent the old shepherd for the midwife, but it took hours for her to get there. Or so it seemed. I don't really know how long it took. I was out of my mind with fright."

"And the baby?" Sarah whispered.

Jane's tears spilled over. She swiped at them with a trembling hand. "When Madame Couteau saw him, she shook her head and said he was dead before my pains started. 'This one was never meant to breathe,' she said."

Sarah leaned over and tucked a handkerchief in Jane's hand.

Jane wiped her cheeks with it. "She asked me if I wanted to send for the priest, and I said no. It was too far, and anyway, I didn't like the thought of having him come around." She shivered. "He always made me feel worthless. He knew that in my heart I kept my 'heretical' beliefs, I suppose."

"Heretical?" Sarah's eyes widened.

"I would not give up being a Protestant."

"Ah."

"The midwife took the baby . . . took him out of the room. I just cried until I went to sleep. Later I woke up, and Madame Couteau told me she had buried him. And so far as I know, she never told anyone, nor did I. It was considered very bad, to bury him without the priest. But I prayed at his grave many times and asked God to forgive me if I did wrong."

Sarah left her chair and put her arms around Jane. "My poor, dear Jane. You didn't do wrong."

"I hope not."

"So Robataille found out when he came home?"

"Yes. He thundered and screamed. He'd been drinking, of course. He always stopped in town with his friends on the way home and had some liquor. He was very angry, and he said it was all my fault that his child was dead. I ought to have kept myself strong enough to bear a healthy child. Not only that, but I hadn't seen that his son had a Christian burial."

"Oh, Jane."

"And of course, the crops weren't in. I'd been ill for weeks afterward, and I couldn't work. The old shepherd had got some men to come for a few days, but it wasn't nearly enough. The wheat was rotting in the field."

"And your husband misused you again."

"Aye. I was so bruised I could barely get about to make his meals. And I never . . . There were no more babies after that. I wondered if things had gone so wrong inside me that I couldn't. Of course, Monsieur Robataille railed about it now and again. He'd made a bad bargain and got a lazy, barren wife. But the next spring he went off again, and he never came back."

"He died on his voyage?"

"Aye. They told me he was drunk and fell overboard and drowned. I believe it. They brought him home to the village, and I let the priest bury him in the churchyard." Jane rested her head against Sarah's shoulder. "I've never told anyone how it was with him. No one. Only you."

"But you must tell Charlie."

"No, I can't." Sobs wracked her body.

Sarah held her, smoothing Jane's hair as she cried.

Jane let the misery of those weeks and months alone take over for a few minutes, feeling guilty even as she cried. Jacques Robataille was not a man worth crying over, and she didn't regret being ransomed from that bitter life. So why was she weeping now? She had landed in a much better situation, and she ought to rejoice. But she couldn't stop sobbing.

When she quieted at last, Sarah said, "You don't think Charlie should know all this?"

Jane drew a ragged breath and squared her shoulders. "I suppose you think it wasn't fair of me not to tell him before we wed. But I didn't. And now . . ."

A fresh wave of guilt washed over her. Had she married Charles under false pretenses? Of course a young man like him wanted children and expected to have them. She met Sarah's gaze. "If it looks like I can't carry another child for him, I will tell him. But I hope . . ."

"What, dear?"

"Well, I wonder if I'm not with child now."

Sarah drew back and stared at her. "Now? But, Jane! This is good news."

"Is it?" Jane felt a new tear trickle down her face. "I'm frightened, Sarah. What if I can't carry a healthy child?"

"But Charlie won't work you to death or

hit you! Of course you can have a healthy baby now."

"Maybe." Jane dabbed at her eyes. "But . . . it might turn out like the last time. There's a lot of pain in childbearing anyway, but there's more pain, and sorrow, too, if things don't go right." She couldn't help picturing the little grave in the windswept pasture back in Quebec. "Forgive me. I'm just so fearful that perhaps I can't give Charles what he wants most. But if I can —" She darted a quick look at Sarah's trusting face. "You mustn't tell him yet. Or Richard, either. Not until I'm sure. Please, Sarah."

"All right. But I hope it's true, and we'll both have babies next winter. Jane, you have to promise me . . ."

"What?"

"That if something goes wrong, you will tell him, so he can fetch me right away for you."

Jane nodded, feeling a bit nauseous just to think of the agony she'd endured that other time. "I pray that I don't go through that again."

Sarah grasped both her hands. "So do I. But if the worst happens, I'll be at your side. And Charlie won't be hundreds of miles away with a bateau crew, trading and drinking while you suffer. He'll be there with you."

Jane sobbed, and Sarah hugged her close again. "I'm sorry. I shouldn't have said that."

Heavy footsteps sounded outside, and Sarah leaped up. "Oh my! Richard is here for dinner. Where has the morning gone?"

"I must go. Charles will want a meal, as well, and I've overstayed my welcome." Jane bounded out of the chair and pulled her shawl on as Richard and his younger brother, Stephen, came in. She hoped they wouldn't notice her puffy red eyes.

Eleven

A week later, Charles sold the last of his furs from the season. He sent them with the trader on a ship to Boston. Four days after that the trader brought him his profit.

Charles left Jane at the Dudley garrison while he went to the village with Richard. All morning, Sarah and Jane quilted with Goody Dudley and Richard's sister, Catherine.

When the men returned, Catherine ran out to open the gate for them at Richard's shout.

Charles came in grinning and handed a small leather pouch to Richard's father. "I thank you again, Goodman Dudley. You helped Jane and me at a time when we needed it sorely."

James weighed the pouch in his hand then set it on the mantel. "Thank you, Charles. I could wait a bit, if you've need of the money for other things."

"Nay," Charles said quickly. "This squares my debt, and now Jane and I are able to go on unencumbered." He looked Jane in the eye and nodded.

She felt her face flush, and she looked down, crumpling her apron in her hands. The furs had sold for enough to discharge the debt. She never should have doubted Charles.

"Come, wife," he said. "My pack is outside. I've brought you a few things. We'll live small until harvest, but we'll get by and be happy."

"Of course we shall," Jane said. She wove her needle into a scrap of cloth and put it in her basket, with the half dozen fresh eggs and small cake of maple sugar Richard's mother had pressed upon her. "Thank you so much, Goody Dudley. Catherine, come visit me soon."

Sarah kissed her cheek. "I'll see you tomorrow."

Richard opened the door and held it for Jane, grinning as though he knew something hilarious.

She eyed him and sidled past him down the step. Charles came behind her, and she felt his steady hand on her elbow as she descended to the yard.

Yip! Something brown and furry jumped

up from the ground beside his pack and let out a fierce bark.

She jumped back, and Charles's arm clamped about her waist.

"What, scared of a half-grown puppy, Wife?"

She stared at the little brown dog. Its nose trembled, and its tail curled high over its back. It stood with all four feet planted, glaring at her and snarling menacingly in its throat, as though it would guard Charles's pack with its very life. She laughed. "He's only a baby."

"Aye. And needs some training. Are you up to the task?"

"I'm not sure. Will you help me?"

"Of course. I couldn't buy you a musket, but Captain Baldwin let me have this pup for a song. Perhaps the dog will bring you a little measure of security. Oh, and I've bartered for a few chickens, too. I'll fetch them home tomorrow."

Charles untied a rope from the strap of his pack, and Jane saw that the other end was fixed in a firm loop around the dog's neck. Her husband turned and waved at Richard and his family. "Farewell, Dudleys. And beware when you approach our cabin that we now have a fierce protector."

■ ■ ■ ■

Two days later, Charles answered Richard's call to help him raise the gate in his new stockade. Stephen also came to help with the chore.

The gate was made, and the hinges set on it. All the three needed to do was hoist it into place.

"Be sure you fix some sort of lock on it," Charles said, "else the enemy would be able to remove the gate as easily as we put it in place."

"Aye," said Richard. "I've iron bolts to drive into place above each hinge, once we've raised it."

They put their strength into lifting the gate of heavy oak and positioning it. Then they let the pins on the hinges fall into place. Richard placed his ladder next to the gatepost and climbed it. Charles stood below to hand him his tools.

"You've finished this none too soon," Stephen said when his brother climbed down again.

"I know it."

"You think the Algonquin tribes will molest us again this summer?" Charles asked.

A dark look passed between Richard and Stephen.

"What?" Charles asked. "You know something."

"I was hunting yesterday," Stephen said. "Two warriors surprised me in the woods, up near the falls."

"Have they come down to fish?"

"Aye. But more than that."

Charles passed the hammer from one hand to the other. "All right. What?"

"These were two St. Francois men," Stephen said.

"That's the tribe you were with last, up in Quebec?"

"I spent nearly four years with them. They are closely related to the Pennacooks Sarah lived with."

Charles nodded. The Pennacook and Saco tribes of the Abenaki confederacy had united to burn the village of Cochecho in 1689 and had killed nearly half the inhabitants. About thirty whites were carried off captive, with himself, Stephen, Sarah, and Jane among them.

"Sarah was adopted by a Pennacook woman," Stephen went on. "The tribe is dwindling. They sold some of their captives to the French. I ended up with their cousins, the St. Francois, farther to the north."

"But you came back." Charles well recalled the desperate trip he and Richard had made into Canada to try to find Stephen.

"I did. But they were not happy. I had pledged to stay with my Indian family, and I fully intended to do so. But after seeing Richard again . . ." Stephen cleared his throat. "I had to sneak away, or they would not have let me leave."

"And now they've found you again."

"Aye. They know I'm living here with my parents again."

Charles took a deep breath and turned to Richard. "Are we all in danger?"

"Perhaps."

Charles nodded. "Have you told Sarah?"

"Not yet. I wanted to finish the stockade first. I'll tell her tonight."

"You say they're camped at the falls. That's only twelve miles from here." Charles looked toward the river, but the intervening woods hid it from view. "What can we do?"

"I told my father," Stephen said. "He doesn't wish to fort up in the village. He thinks we can defend his garrison if necessary."

Charles shook his head. "They burned five garrisons that night."

"We know," Richard said. "Do you think

we should all move into town? Take up residence at Otises' or Heards' garrison until they've left?"

Charles considered that. It might be safer to stay for a while at one of the larger compounds, but he didn't want to neglect his farm and sit idle in another man's house. "No. Unless . . ." He looked keenly at Stephen. "These warriors were men you knew?"

Stephen nodded.

"What did they say to you?"

"That I had betrayed their family. Their aunt had adopted me, and they said her heart was broken when I left. They said they could have killed me right then, but that would only make her grieve more."

"Did they ask you to go back to the tribe?"

"Not in so many words."

Richard picked up the ladder. "Come, boys, let's put these things away. I'm sure Charles doesn't want to leave Jane alone long."

"They didn't seem in a warlike mood," Stephen said, swinging the gate shut behind them. He put the two bars in place.

"They wouldn't come after you, would they?" Richard asked.

"I don't think they would force me to go back."

"I don't like them being so close," Charles said.

Stephen shrugged. "They come every year."

"I know."

Stephen chuckled a bit sheepishly. "I came with them once, three summers ago."

"What?" Richard dropped the ladder against the inside wall of the stockade and stared at him. "You came that close to home, and we didn't know it?"

"Just that one time. I was tempted to come over here, but they watched me. And at that time I was confused. I didn't think I was, but now I can see that it's true. I thought the Indian way was better, and I didn't wish to live the white way again."

Charles refused to dwell on that or to wonder what the lad would have done if the Indians had raided his father's house that summer. "But now?" He eyed Stephen anxiously. "You wouldn't go back to them now, would you, Stephen? Your mother —"

Stephen shook his head. "Nay, I am here for good. I have made my peace with God. And I shall not hunt anymore while the tribe is at the falls. I've no wish to meet them again."

Charles pondered that. Should he tell Jane? He didn't want to alarm her. They were about to plant their crops. He would be extra careful and not let her work in the field alone. He would stay closer to home than he had been of late. Uneasily, he glanced at the sky and saw that the sun was high overhead. "I must go home."

"You can take dinner with us," Richard said. "I'm sure Sarah has cooked enough."

"Nay. Thank you, but I don't think I'll leave Jane alone any longer."

Jane's back ached as she bent to drop bean seeds in the furrow. Charles came behind her with his hoe, covering the seeds over and tamping the earth. All afternoon he had trudged along the rows with his musket slung over his shoulder and his hoe in his hands.

The dog, which Jane had named Samson, trotted about the field, sniffing here and there, snapping at bugs, but he always returned to Charles. As they neared the end of a row, he galloped toward them and plopped down in the loose earth at Charles's feet. He stared up at his master, tail wagging, with a pathetically wistful expression on his face. Charles laughed aloud and stooped to pet him. Samson woofed and ran off again to explore the brush pile at the corner of the field.

Jane feared Samson was too friendly to make a good watchdog, but somehow Charles seemed to have gotten across to him that Gardners were good and anyone else approaching the homestead was suspect and therefore worthy of much noise and ferocity. The dog had scared Sarah when she visited, jumping toward her with his teeth bared, halted only by the chain that held him tethered to the barn wall. But inside the house he was gentle, and Charles encouraged Jane to spoil him just a bit so that he would love her.

"You be the one to feed him," Charles had told her. "If you pet him regularly when you give him his feed, he'll be your slave. He'll go with you when you want to go to Sarah's or Catherine's, and if you meet anyone, he'll stand and protect you."

"What can he do?" Jane had asked. "He's only a youngster."

"He'll grow yet. And don't let his size fool you. If you win him over, you'll have his loyalty, and he'll defend you tooth and nail."

And so she did as Charles said. She fed Samson special treats but didn't urge him to befriend the neighbors.

At the end of the row, she straightened, shoving her fists into her lower back and watching Charles finish covering the seeds with soil.

"What now?" she asked. "More beans?"

Charles squinted up at the sky. The sun had sunk behind the trees edging their field. "You've done enough for one day. I shall plant another row while you go and put our supper on the table."

She nodded. "It shan't take me very long. I left the stew simmering."

Charles had killed a feral pig a few days earlier, and they'd dined on pork and shared a roast with the Dudleys. It pleased Jane to be the one giving the portion of meat. Sarah had come to help Jane try out the lard, a job the women usually did at fall butchering time. But Jane didn't mind. The nights were still cool enough to keep the meat from spoiling quickly. Having fresh meat in late May was a luxury, and she could see that her husband enjoyed it, too.

Her sore muscles protested as she plodded to the house. She couldn't think of it as a cabin anymore. It was too fine for that now, with the two large rooms and the luxurious pantry, though most of its shelves were still bare.

The small barn was complete now, too, and Charles was confident they would soon be able to buy a heifer and a few sheep. The half dozen chickens he had bartered for tottered about the yard, scratching for insects, as she approached the door. Their farm was on its way to prosperity.

And their family would increase. She was almost sure now. Not that she would let herself rejoice until she felt the baby kick. That would be the sign that all was well, and then she would tell Charles. She knew he would be pleased. She could almost see his contented smile as he sorted through the hardwood logs he had cut and set aside to dry, hunting for just the right wood from which to build his son's cradle. And she would stitch a flannel gown for her own babe and embroider it all over with rosebuds.

Samson came and thrust his nose into her palm. She petted him, and he turned and ran back toward the garden where Charles still worked.

Jane went into the dim house and hung up her shawl. She found herself humming a psalm as she swung the crane out from the fireplace, getting her stew pot out of the way, and poked up the fire. Charles had been so good to her, she would like to give him the gift of a child. A son he could teach to hunt and fish and farm.

Yesterday she'd almost told him when he came in from planting corn and found her napping in the middle of the morning. She was so tired all the time. Today she'd made an effort to hide her fatigue and keep up with Charles as they planted the garden. She didn't want him to feel she couldn't work at his side when he needed her.

Their relationship was entirely different from the one she'd had with Jacques Robataille. She'd felt like a slave those three years. Monsieur Robataille told her what to do then went away. If he returned and found things weren't done to his satisfaction, he made her pay for it.

Charlie, on the other hand, borrowed James Dudley's oxen to plow his field. He put the bag of seeds in Jane's hand and followed her step by step down the rows, covering the beans and peas that she dropped, watching over her all the time. And at night he came in for his supper exhausted and thanked her for cooking it.

Yes, things were very different with Charles than they had been on the farm in Quebec. Could things get any better, she wondered? More to the point, was there anything she could do personally to make things better for the man who treated her so well?

Aye, she told herself. *You can tell him he'll be a father next winter, and that will make him the happiest man in the colony.*

But if I tell him, and then I find out it isn't really so . . .

No, it was so. It had to be. The morning nausea she'd only just overcome, the aching muscles, the chronic fatigue, the missing cycle. Sarah insisted it was true. A child was growing inside her. Sarah also badgered her to tell her husband.

Nay, better wait a little while longer, just in case.

Jane stirred up the dough for fresh biscuits. The new lard would make up for the lack of milk and the flat taste of last year's flour. She hurried to get the biscuits cooking in the Dutch oven.

Her heart lifted as she heard Charles's firm step at the door. While he came in and hung up his hat, she poured hot water in the basin and added some cold; then she laid the pannikin of soft soap and a linen towel beside it.

The small tasks she performed for her husband added a sweetness to the day. She was tired, yes, but she didn't mind that. Being here with Charles in their home and knowing their labor would produce food to sustain them through the year brought her a great satisfaction. In fact, her present contentment was deeper than any she had known before.

He smiled at her as he dried his calloused hands, and Jane found herself smiling back at him.

His eyes glinted and he leaned toward her, across her worktable, and tucked a wisp of her hair behind her ear. "I like to see you happy, wife."

"I *am* happy, Charles."

A smile of true delight spread over his face, making her glad that she had told him.

"I think we shall have a good year together," he said.

"Aye, we've made a good start on our garden, and you say we shall have some stock soon."

He nodded thoughtfully, and she realized he spoke of things less tangible than the crops. But it was still difficult to talk about those things. She would work on it.

"Is everything ready?" he asked.

"Aye."

He went to the table. Jane followed, carrying a dish of butter that Richard's mother had brought on her visit a few days past.

Outside, Samson began to bark. Jane looked at Charles in inquiry.

"Did you hitch him by the barn?"

"Nay, he was chasing a squirrel when I came in. He probably wants his supper."

Charles started to rise, but Jane was already on her feet, so she strode toward the door. She passed one of the tall, narrow windows and peered out to see if she could catch a glimpse of the dog. But Samson was out of sight, still barking. She opened the front door and looked toward the sound.

As she leaned out, his barking stopped. She saw a dark figure in the dusk. At once she recognized the hairstyle and buckskin garb of an Algonquin warrior. Her heart seemed to stop for in instant as the Indian bent over the body of her little mongrel dog. The warrior looked up, his dark eyes settling on her.

Twelve

Jane gasped and ducked inside, slammed the door, and groped for the bar. "Charlie! Quick!"

Charles leaped from his chair. "What is it?"

"Indians!"

Her husband was at her side, sliding the heavy bar into place and slipping the two iron hooks he'd installed at the top and bottom of the oak door into their staples. As soon as the door was secure, he stepped to the corner where he had left his musket leaning a few minutes earlier. "Where are they?" he asked.

"I only saw one, just beyond the east corner of the barn. He's killed Samson, I fear."

"Get my bullet pouch and powder horn."

Jane rushed to grab them from the shelf beside his leather working tools.

"Now put up the shutters in the bedchamber." Charles slung the strap of the powder horn over his neck.

Jane ran to the other room and quickly raised the shutters, turning the wooden blocks that held them in place. The room became pitch dark, and she groped her way back to the doorway.

Charles had closed all the shutters but one in the keeping room and was staring through the slot that looked out on the barn.

"Do you see them?"

"Nay." He glanced at her. "That dog saved our lives, I've no doubt."

Jane gritted her teeth. "Well, they aren't saved yet."

"Are you certain of what you saw? I mean . . . it couldn't have been Stephen Dudley, could it?"

"He wore buckskins, and his hair hung down in a long lock. Stephen cut his hair and has put off his Algonquin clothing."

"Aye, it's true."

"Besides, Samson would still be barking if it were Stephen come to call. And Stephen would have come to the door by now."

"I fear you are right. I only hoped there might be a mistake."

A sudden *thunk* on the roof caused both Charles and Jane to look upward.

"Something hit the roof," Jane said.

Charles tightened his grasp on the stock of his musket. "Pray that it's not a fire arrow."

"The shingles . . ."

"Will not catch as readily as thatch would, but those on the front of the house are seasoned and dry."

"Charles!" She stepped toward him and stopped. Panicking would not help. "Think you they will burn the house around us?"

"They might."

She shivered. "Why are they so quiet? When they attacked Major Waldron's, they shrieked and howled."

"He saw you when you looked out. They've lost the element of surprise. But still —"

A missile whizzed in through the window slit, narrowly missing Charles's ear, and tore through the air between them. It struck the stone fireplace opposite and clattered to the floor. A scream stuck in Jane's throat as she stared down at the shattered arrow.

Charles looked at her in the dimness for an instant; then he whirled once more to the narrow window and peered out into the twilight.

"Charles, don't!"

He flattened himself against the wall beside the aperture. "Would you have me put up the shutters and wait for them to burn us out?"

She gulped and nudged the arrow with her toe. "Is it Pennacook? Can you tell?"

"Bring it here."

She picked up the end with the fletching and took it to him, staying clear of the line of fire through the window.

Charles held up the broken shaft, examining the feather work. "One of the Algonquin tribes, anyway. But they're all kin. The tribes could join together, as the Saco and Pennacook did at the massacre six years ago." He shook his head. "Either the archer was right outside the window, or that was an incredibly fortunate shot. The opening is only three inches wide." He drew Jane closer to the wall and held her against him for a moment. "I'm sorry, dear wife."

Breathing was suddenly a chore, and she wished she could stay sheltered in his arms forever. But she pulled away from him and straightened her shoulders. "Can't you speak to them? Tell them you are a friend?"

"Am I?"

She hesitated, not sure of his meaning. "You lived with them. You know their language."

"I don't think they consider me their friend anymore, dearest. I escaped them and

215

ran back to my own people. When Richard and I went looking for Stephen, we were not treated as friends."

"But still, Charlie! Might it not give them pause to hear you speak in their own tongue?"

Still he stood unmoving.

A chilling scream split the night. Jane dove into his arms.

"These may be men I hunted and raided with a few years ago," Charles said softly, his lips against her hair. "What would I tell them? I'll never go back to their ways. And I shall not open the door and invite them to supper, Jane."

"Do you wish me to go into the bedchamber and look out the back?"

"I should hate for you to expose yourself."

Another arrow thunked against the wall outside the window.

Jane raised her chin. "I won't be captured again, Charles."

He nodded. "Then we need to know how many they are and where. I'll let the fire die out. If you see any flicker of light outside or smell smoke or hear a crackle of flame, you tell me."

"Aye. They couldn't come in through the chimney, could they?"

"Nay, it's too small. There's one loophole

up in the loft yonder. I'll climb up and see if I can see anything from there. Mayhap they won't look up and I can surprise them."

"Do be careful." She crept through the bedroom door and cautiously lowered the shutter on the window nearest the bed, crouching beneath the casement. When nothing happened, she straightened beside it and leaned over for a quick glance outside. It was now so dark that she could see little. The trees at the edge of the clearing waved, and a breeze soughed through the branches.

Jane shivered. She wished she had grabbed her butcher knife as she left the kitchen. She stared out into the night, keeping to one side just in case a savage should fire point-blank at the window slit.

She heard Charles moving in the other room, then a rustling behind her. She turned. A shadow filled the doorway, and he spoke.

"I couldn't see them from above, and I've put up all the shutters for now. Can you see anything?"

"Nay. But it's windy, and I can't tell for sure. They could be out there at the tree line."

"Then we may as well shut this one." He raised the plank cover and fixed it in place. "Jane, there's something I must tell you."

"What?"

"Stephen told me yesterday that there were Algonquin at the falls."

Her heart stopped for a moment; then it raced. "Why didn't you tell me? We spent the whole day out planting!"

"I thought we were safe. He said they were a Canadian tribe, come down to fish."

"Were they the ones he knew?"

"Aye."

"He spoke to them?"

"Two of their men surprised him in the woods."

She caught her breath. "They didn't hurt him?"

"Nay. But they let him know they were not pleased he had left them."

"I wish you had told me."

He sighed. "I didn't wish to alarm you."

She nodded. "Well, it seems they want something now."

"Probably food and other plunder."

Suddenly a loud thumping came on the door, and the whole house shivered. She threw herself into his arms.

"Charles! We mustn't let them break through! I tell you, I shall not go with them, whatever it costs me."

Slowly he pulled her arms from around his waist. In the dim light, she saw his grim expression.

"Here. Take my skinning knife." He pressed the hilt into her hand. "Get into the pantry and lock yourself in. I shall go up into the loft again. It overhangs a few inches above the door, and there is a small hole in the floor. If they're at the door, I might be able to shoot one of them."

"I shall come with you and reload for you."

"Nay, Jane. Lock yourself in. Do not open the door for anyone but me. But please, my love, if they burn the house . . ."

"Go quickly," she gasped.

He left her.

She squeezed the bone handle of his knife and drew in a deep breath. It was only a few steps to the door of the bedchamber. She felt along the wall to the door of the pantry. Inside the small storeroom, she fumbled with the latch. She hadn't noticed before that he had put two sturdy bars on the inside of the door. Jane struggled to fit them into place.

In the darkness, she knelt on the floor. *Please, dear God, save me and my husband!*

Charles bounded to the ladder and up again into the loft. His father had added it over one end of the main room of the cabin years ago. The upper part of the house stuck out over the front door. It wasn't as pronounced as in the larger garrison houses, but it gave enough leeway for him to cut a hole in the floor just over the front door. Most of the garrison houses in the area were built with the chimney in the middle and the upper story jutting out over the lower one all around, enabling the inhabitants to fire down on people outside. The Gardner house was not nearly so convenient, but Charles was thankful for what little advantage he had.

As he gained the loft, the front door shuddered again, and he was afraid for a moment the hinges would give. He ducked his head and hurried across to the one narrow window. Lowering the shutter, he looked out but couldn't see what was going on below. He had a clear view, however, along the path toward Richard's home. No light was visible. The new fence around the Dudley house might obscure illumination from within the building, he thought. At least the place wasn't on fire.

He felt along the edge of the wall and located the hole his father had made in the floor. Peering through it, he had an impression of confused movement, and another loud thud jarred the house. He'd thought they were ramming the door with a log, but now he wasn't so sure. Perhaps they were attacking the oak planks with a hatchet. A sickening thought hit him. He'd left his ax in the barn, and they might be using his own tools against him.

He stuck the barrel of his musket into the hole and waited. He could barely see past it, and he didn't want to waste his shot. He might get only one. It would take him a minute or two to reload. That delay might be enough time to let them gain entrance to the house. The first shot had to count.

There came a pause in the chopping sounds. He heard them muttering, and then the *thud-thud* resumed. He thought the movement he saw was the ax, swung by a dusky arm. He didn't want to hit one of them in the arm. He wanted a clean, fatal shot. And so he waited, holding his breath.

Suddenly a light flared, and he knew they had ignited a torch. A loud crack told him one of the planks of the door gave way, and a dark body shoved against the door. Charles pulled the trigger.

At once he wished he'd put wool in his ears. The report of the gun in the enclosed space deafened him for several seconds, and acrid smoke brought tears to his eyes. He crawled to the window loop and put his face to the slit, gulping in fresh air. Slowly his hearing returned, though his ears rang with an ongoing tone that muffled the sounds from below. A soft glow told him the torch still burned, and the Indians were yelling in outrage.

He groped his way back to the hole in the floor and peeked through it. Nothing. He put his mouth close to the opening and yelled, in the Algonquin language, "Go away! I shall kill you all if you do not go away!"

He jumped back away from the hole and fumbled in the darkness to begin the reloading process. He hoped Richard had heard his musket fire and received a warning. Or was it too late? Was this small raiding party one of many?

He couldn't help remembering that awful night six years ago, when four hundred warriors had attacked the settlement, killing or capturing half the colonists. Everyone in the colony measured time by that event. "The year before the massacre . . ."

He dropped a bullet and felt about for it in the dark. Rather than waste more time searching for it, he reached into his pouch for another.

The chopping at the door began again.

THIRTEEN

In the dark pantry, Jane huddled in a corner and prayed. She jumped when a gun fired. That had to be her husband's musket. The repercussion rang in her ears, but she had heard no firearms outside.

All was quiet for a minute, and she heard voices. Then the pounding began again. *They must be battering the door.* How terrible this waiting was!

She remembered that other time, when her mistress had yanked her out of bed. *"Quick! Put your skirt on. There be savages at the door."*

Jane hadn't even had time to don her overskirt that night. The roof of Waldrons' garrison was already ablaze. She grabbed her clothing and ran. Indians had caught them as they fled from the fire. Her mistress was tomahawked on the doorstep. Jane had hung back in terror, but strong hands had seized her and pulled her from the blazing building. Instead of killing her, they had dragged her outside the stockade and bound her with several others to await the end of their captors' bloody business. Then the long march began.

She shivered and hugged her flexed knees, holding tight to the knife's hilt.

God, help us! Help my Charlie! Send us aid, Lord!

What would she do if they killed Charles and discovered her hiding place? The idea was too terrible to consider. Feverishly she renewed her prayers.

Crack! The musket fired again.

She jumped and stared toward the door she couldn't see. Charles was still fighting them off. She needed to be beside him. If they killed him, her life was worth nothing. She and their baby would die or be herded off to Canada again, and sold to the French or made to live with the savages as Sarah and Stephen had been.

She scrambled up and groped for the door. In the darkness, she threw off the bar at waist level then reached for the one above.

The stillness stopped her. No one was yelling. No one was pounding on the front door. No gunfire. No *thwack* of arrows against the stout walls.

She heard a muffled thud then unmistakable footsteps. Her husband? Or the enemy? Indians would not wear hard-soled boots. Her heart pounded, but she dared not open the door.

"Jane?"

She almost collapsed, so great was her relief. She grasped the upper bar and stood on tiptoe to throw it out of its niche. The end of it fell down and whacked her forearm. She let it fall to the floor with a clatter and stood clutching her bruised arm.

"Jane?"

The door creaked open.

"Charlie!"

He pulled her into his embrace, resting the stock of his musket on the floor. "Are you all right?" he asked.

"Yes. Are you?"

"Aye."

"Are they gone?"

"I think so. I saw shadows retreating toward the woods."

"Did you reload?"

He laughed and hugged her tighter. "Aye, wife. I'd have been here sooner, otherwise."

She squeezed him with all her might. She would rather have died here and now than to carry Charles's baby into Canada and give birth there. But this third option was far sweeter.

"What happened?"

"I haven't opened the front door, what's left of it. But I'm pretty sure I hit two of them. The rest gave up."

Her hairpins had come loose, and her hair had come unbound and spilled over her shoulders. Charles held her and stroked her long tresses and planted a kiss on the top of her head. "Come. We must warn Richard and the others."

"You can't leave me here alone!"

He hesitated. "Nay, I shan't. They perhaps heard my shooting. But, Jane, we can't take the chance that the warriors left here to attack another house."

"Then fire your gun out the window. Charlie, you mustn't go out! You'll be killed."

"It's possible," he acknowledged. "Would you really mind so much being widowed again?"

She stared at him, able to see only his glittering eyes. A huge sob worked its way up her throat. Did he think she cared nothing for him? She threw herself back into his arms and wept.

Of all the crackbrained things he'd ever said in his life, this had to be the worst. Charles held his wife, not knowing what else to do.

It seemed her crying would never end. Her tears soaked the front of his linsey-woolsey shirt.

"Jane, my love, I'm so sorry. Forgive me."

She sobbed harder. Her arms circled his rib cage, squeezing the breath out of him. He managed to lean the musket against the shelves in the corner and slid down to the floor, taking her with him. He pulled her onto his lap, leaned against the door frame, and let her weep.

At last her sobs slowed, and she gulped great gasps of air between them. Her lush hair swirled about her face as her shoulders heaved.

He patted her back with one hand and pushed her hair away from her face with the other. "I'm sorry," he whispered. "That was thoughtless of me. Can you forgive me?"

She nodded vigorously and sobbed again. He cradled her into a more comfortable position, sheltering her in his arms.

After a long moment, she sat up, wiping her eyes with her apron. "If you must go to see if Richard is well, Charlie, so be it. I shall barricade myself and wait for you to return. But I warn you, I shall never forgive you if you leave me here to raise your son without a father."

Charles sat very still. He wished desperately for a candle in that moment so he could see her face. "My . . . son?"

"Or daughter. Girls need their fathers, as well, you know."

"Is this . . . something I should know, Wife? Or are you merely hypostatizing?"

She sniffed. "If I knew what that meant, I would answer."

He chuckled. "I heard the parson say it. It means you're advancing a theory."

She laid her head on his chest. "I assure you, sir, this baby is not theoretical. It's early, but I'm sure I felt him kick as the savages beat on our door."

Charles inhaled deeply, letting the joyous warmth creep over him.

Her small, warm hands crept up about his neck once more. "Are you pleased, Husband?"

"More than I can tell you."

She ran her fingers into his beard and stroked his cheek.

He pulled her to him and kissed her.

A sharp rapping on the door startled them apart.

Jane clenched handfuls of his shirt in her fists. "They're back!"

"Nay. They would not be so polite. Hear that?"

They both listened and heard an anxious

voice calling, "Charlie! Charlie! Are you in there, man? Open up if you are!"

"Richard," Jane breathed.

Charles stood and braced himself against the doorjamb so he could pull her to her feet.

"Let me get a candle," she said.

"No time."

Charles hurried across the dark keeping room. "Hold on, Richard!"

Jane groped about the pantry for a candle as she heard him unfastening the door. Her hand closed on a tin holder with the stub of a tallow candle in it. She seized it and hurried out to the fireplace in the other room.

"Charlie, we heard you shoot, and Stephen and I thought we'd best come make sure you were all right. What happened?"

As her husband explained their brief siege, Jane probed the ashes in the fireplace with the poker and found a few red coals. She held her candle stub to one and soon had a light. She used the flame to light two more on the mantel and carried one to Charles.

He took it from her and raised it to aid him in examining the damaged door.

"A few more blows, and they'd have been in the house," Richard said.

"Aye. So it seems." Charles ran his hand over the broken planks.

"They nearly had you. Why did they leave?"

"I shot a couple of them. See that?" He held the candle over the doorstep, and they saw a dark smear on the flat granite stone. "That's blood. I've a little hole in the loft floor. It gave me just enough room to shoot through. I believe I seriously wounded or killed two of them."

"They've taken their friends away," Richard observed, peering about the yard.

"Come in." Charles stepped back and let the brothers enter.

Jane hurried back to the hearth, took some pinecones from her tinderbox, and laid them on the coals. By adding a few small sticks of kindling, she soon had a good blaze going.

"You must stay at our house tonight," Richard said.

"It would be better if you all, including Sarah, come over to Father's," Stephen said.

"You think they will come back?" Charles asked. "Could they have gone for reinforcements?"

Stephen shrugged. "I doubt it. The encampment at the falls was a small one. But you never know, and it's many hours until daylight."

"Safety in numbers," Richard agreed.

"Jane, grab your cloak and a blanket or two."

"We've not even had our supper," she protested. "I was about to feed my husband when the attack began."

Richard laughed. "Then cover your stew pot, and we'll bring it along."

"Hold, now," said Charles. "I'm not sure I want to go and leave my house unprotected. If I'm not here to defend it, they could return and plunder everything."

"How many did you see?" Stephen asked.

"I didn't actually see much, I tell you. I wasn't about to open the door, and my windows don't afford much of a view, unfortunately. But from the sound of things —"

"It sounded like a legion of them," Jane said.

Charles chuckled. "Nay, there weren't many, or they'd have been all around the house and shooting faster. I think there were only a few. Certainly not more than half a dozen of them, perhaps fewer."

Stephen eyed the scarred door again. "Maybe in the morning we should gather a delegation of men from the village and go up to the falls. Pay them a visit and let them know we won't put up with this sort of thing."

"I don't know," Richard said. "When they

came six years ago, they had four hundred warriors. What if they gather a swarm like that again and retaliate?"

"Well, we can't just live out here on the edge of the wilderness in terror every minute," Jane said. She fitted the cover on her stew kettle and handed it to Charles.

He studied her face. "Perhaps we should move into the village — for the summer, at least. A lot of people do that. Live in town and walk out here to work their fields."

But Jane raised her chin. "Nay, Husband. We'll not let them run us off. Your father claimed this land, and Gardner land it shall be. As you said, if we leave the house empty, they are more apt to pillage. And you've just built me that fine new addition. I'll go with you this one night to Goodman Dudley's garrison, but tomorrow morning we return."

Pride swelled in Charles's chest at her words.

"You speak well. But I think my next building project should be a stockade." He turned to the Dudley brothers. "Are you willing to help me?"

Richard and Stephen gave their assent, and the four left the little house.

As they walked toward the path that led to Richard's house, Jane stared about at the starlit yard. "Charlie! I believe they stole our chickens."

"That would not surprise me. I believe they got my ax, as well."

"Impudent scoundrels!"

Charles reached for her hand. Indeed, he had chosen the right woman.

Jane was grateful for her neighbors' hospitality, but by morning she was anxious to return to her own home. At first light she was up and helping Goody Dudley prepare a hearty breakfast for them all. But she was to be disappointed. The young men insisted on walking to the village to enlist the aid of the elders in dealing with the Indians. Sarah and Jane stayed with Richard's parents and his sister, Catherine, while Charles undertook the mission with Stephen and Richard.

"You are restless, Jane," Goody Dudley said an hour after the young men had left. "Did you bring your fancywork?"

"Nay, I didn't think to bring anything but my kettle and a quilt," Jane said.

"Then put your hand to the spinning wheel. You shall have all the woolen yarn you can spin this morning."

"Oh no, that is too generous, but I shall spin for you." Jane approached the large wheel in the corner of the main room.

"Nonsense." Her hostess came over and opened a large sack of carded wool. "James and Richard have finished the first shearing, and we look to have a good crop of wool this year. In fact, Charles was speaking to my husband about bartering for a couple of lambs."

Goodman Dudley nodded. "After your Charlie has a stockade built, I'll let him have some ewe lambs to start you a flock."

Sarah had brought her knitting, and she sat down near Jane to work, while Catherine and her mother began to set the dough for their week's baking.

"I'll warrant you'll need lots of wool this year to knit wee things, won't you, now?" Goody Dudley said with a smile.

Jane gasped and eyed Sarah suspiciously.

"I didn't say a word. My mother-in-law is canny about these things."

Goody Dudley laughed. "Ah, so my hunch is true. Two new babies on the frontier next winter. Well, I shall stitch you a flannel gown for the babe, Jane."

"Thank you. No one's embroidery is as fine as yours, ma'am."

"And I shall make you a little blanket," Catherine said.

Sarah leaned toward Jane. "Did you tell Charles yet?"

"Aye. Last night, when he proposed leaving me alone to go and warn you about the savages." Jane felt her face flush.

"Good, because my mother-in-law is not known to be close-lipped."

Jane smiled.

An hour later, Richard returned alone.

"Captain Baldwin has mustered thirty men to go with him to the falls," he reported as he took off his coat.

"But where be Stephen and Charles?" asked his father. "Did they go with the captain?"

"Aye, he wanted them to translate."

"Do you think those savages will attack again?" his mother asked.

"What if they have more men than Stephen thought, and they force a confrontation?" Sarah asked in alarm.

Richard shook his head. "Charles's house seems to be the only one they menaced last night. It's distressing, yet if they intended widespread mischief, I think they would have gone elsewhere when Charles ran them off. The captain agrees. He thinks they were a small band out to see if they could make a quick raid for whatever they could plunder."

"You don't think Stephen was the cause, then?" Catherine asked as she lifted a loaf of rye bread from the Dutch oven.

Richard scowled at his sister. "Why do you say that, Cat?"

"You know what he told us. They stopped him in the woods the other day. They know who he is and that he lives nearby. It occurred to me that perhaps they thought Charles's house was his."

Richard looked toward his father. "I don't think so, do you, sir?"

James Dudley frowned. "If they wanted revenge on Stephen, they could have killed him in the woods. Ambushed him anytime they pleased. Nay, I lean toward the captain's notion. Perhaps their fishing has been poor, and they thought to steal some corn and livestock."

"I agree." Richard pinched a small piece of bread from Catherine's loaf, and she swatted at his hand. "This was not a war party. Just an ill-advised venture by some hot-blooded young warriors. Be thankful they didn't burn us all out."

They stayed within the stockade all day. Richard and his father tended the stock and the kitchen garden but did not venture out to the fields.

At last, as the sun dipped behind the trees to the west, Charles and Stephen came to the gate, and Richard let them in.

"They are few," Stephen told them. "Only twelve or so men and their families. They were packing to leave when we got there."

Charles nodded. "One man lay inside a hut. They said he was sick, but I figure he was one I wounded last night."

"And I think you killed one, as well," Stephen said. "They were frightened when they saw our numbers. Of course, the captain told them we have many more men in reserve if they want to make war. They assured us they are peaceful."

"Denied coming near my house," Charles said, "but we know better. I saw the feathers from our chickens, Jane."

"They ate them already?" she cried.

"I'm afraid so."

"They thought they had an easy target at an unfortified house far from the village," Richard said.

"But they've gone now," Stephen said. "We stayed until they broke camp and headed off north."

Jane took their wedding quilt from the chest by the door. "So we shall be safe at our house tonight?"

"I believe so. Are you ready to go?" Charles picked up her kettle and his gun.

No persuasion from Richard's mother could convince them to stay, for Jane was eager to be back in her own house. She realized as they trudged along the path that the farm on the edge of the forest had become her home.

As they came into the dooryard, a hen cackled and flew up from almost beneath Charles's boots.

"What do you know?" he cried. "At least one of our chickens escaped them."

Jane looked around. "I don't see Samson."

"I stopped and buried him on the way back from the falls."

"Good." She'd tried not to think that Indians might have taken him.

"Richard and Stephen shall come in the morning," Charles said as he opened the door to their house. "Perhaps James, as well. They are all agreed we must have a stockade here."

"Charles, you want to stay here, don't you?" She hung her shawl on its peg and hung the kettle on the crane over the cold hearth. "Because I don't want you to do it if you'd rather not."

"Aye, abandoning this place would go against the grain with me. My thoughts were only to keep you safe, Jane."

"Then it's settled. We shall stay."

He smiled and reached inside the front of his shirt, drawing out a small doeskin pouch. "This will help us."

"What is it?"

As he handed it to her, his dark eyes twinkled.

She could tell by its weight and firmness that it held coins. "Where did you get it?"

"Captain Baldwin."

"Whatever for?"

Charles flexed his shoulders as though somewhat bewildered himself. "He gave this to me before we left the village. Said he'd written to the magistrate in Portsmouth about our situation, and the court declared that since Gideon Plaisted had profited from selling your papers to me — and he set a very high value on your labor, you know — why, then, he should reimburse the governor for the ransom that the colony paid for you."

Jane gasped. "They made him pay?"

"Aye, and the governor sent part of the money here, since the village of Cochecho raised much of the ransom. The elders apparently felt some of that should come to me. To *us*, that is. Baldwin said there was an air of justice about it."

She laughed and loosened the thong at the neck of the pouch and poured the coins into her hand. "Why, we could buy the captain's heifer!"

"Yes, we could. I wanted to show you the money first and let you decide how to spend it. Would you like a heifer, Wife? And perhaps a spinning wheel and a sack of wheat flour?"

She trickled the coins carefully back into the little sack. "Do as you think best, Charles. I know you will be wise in your dealings."

He smiled and knelt to build the fire up. As the kindling caught and began to crackle, he said, "It's good to be home. Tomorrow we'll begin building the fence. But my evening job for the next few weeks shall be another building task."

"What is that?" Jane tried to think what he would build next. "Do you mean repairing the door they've chopped to pieces? Or the loom you spoke of making for me?"

"Nay, not those, though I shall fix the door straightaway. But I was thinking of another project. I cut a big cherry tree last fall, and it's drying in the clearing. I didn't know what it was for then, but now I do." His dark eyes gleamed as he stood and reached for her.

"What?" she asked, but she thought she knew.

"A cradle, sweet wife."

She let him kiss her and twined her arms

about his neck, inviting him to linger. "I meant to tell you about it when all was sure and safe," she whispered. "Not when we were like to be killed."

"It's all right." He squeezed her. "I'm glad, no matter how you told me."

"There's something else. I know I should have told it to you before, but I didn't."

He leaned back, a stab of concern in his face. "What is it?"

"Only that I love you, Charlie."

His smile returned, brighter than the glow from the hearth. "Another answered prayer. I love you, dearest Jane."

ABOUT THE AUTHOR

Susan Page Davis and her husband, Jim, have been married thirty-two years and have six children, ages thirteen to thirty. They live in Maine, where they are active in an independent Baptist church. Susan is a homeschooling mother and writes historical romance, mystery, and suspense novels. Visit her Web site at: www.susanpagedavis.com.